Betsy-Tacy and Tib

Betsy-Tacy and Tib

Maud Hart Lovelace

Illustrated by Lois Lenski

HarperTrophy®
A Division of HarperCollins*Publishers*

LC Number 41-18714
ISBN 0-06-024416-X
ISBN 0-06-440097-2 (pbk.)

16 17 18 OPM 30 29 28
First published in hardcover by Thomas Y. Crowell Company in 1941.
First Harper Trophy edition, 1979.

For
MIDGE *and* JOAN

Contents

Foreword

I was ten when I discovered the books about Betsy, Tacy, and Tib. This was years and years ago, in 1965, and even then the stories seemed old-fashioned—in a tantalizing way that sent me hurrying to our school library to see just how many books by Maud Hart Lovelace I might find there.

After reading the first few pages of *Betsy-Tacy*, I remember flipping to the front of the book to check the copyright date. It had been published in 1940, and the other books about Betsy and her friends followed soon after. I made some calculations in my head. In the early 1940s my mother had been young, a high-school student. But surely the adventures of Betsy, Tacy, and Tib were supposed to have taken place long before then. I was right. A talk with my mother revealed that the stories were about girls who were growing up at the time my grandmothers were little. In fact, Granny, my grandmother Adele, was nearly the same age as Maud Hart Lovelace, who wrote the stories about her own childhood. Ms. Lovelace was born in 1892; Granny was born in 1893. And I am fairly certain that my independent, high-spirited grandmother must have had a childhood similar to Betsy Ray's. Never mind that Betsy and her friends lived in Minnesota and my grandmother grew up in Arkansas. As I read about the School Entertainment and ice-cream socials, about ladies leaving calling cards and the milkman with his horse-drawn wagon, I felt that I was having an unexpected and welcome peek into Granny's childhood—a gift to me from Maud Hart Lovelace.

As I continued to read about Betsy and Tacy and Tib, I discovered something equally as wonderful as the fact that the books could have been about my beloved granny. Even though they took place at the turn of the twentieth century, the things that happened in the books were very like some of the things that happened to my parents when they were growing up later, in the 1920s and 1930s. The trouble at the School Entertainment in *Betsy and Tacy Go Over the Big Hill* prompted a story from my father about the time he broke his arm during a school play. I told my mother about Betsy and Tacy and the ornery hen in *Betsy-Tacy*, and she told me about getting in trouble in first grade for letting some visiting chickens out of their cage. These were small stories, things that could happen to anyone, but when Maud Hart Lovelace told small stories she made them seem big.

And, I eventually realized, the small stories were stories that could happen at any time. The more I thought about it, the more I discovered that I liked Betsy and Tacy and Tib because although they were growing up a good seventy years before I was, their lives weren't really so different from mine. My friends and my sister and I were active, independent girls. We staged parades and carnivals and plays. We built things, we planned things, we concocted things. We had big ideas and we carried them out. I could be Betsy, I thought, as I read about choosing a Queen of Summer, or making a house in a piano box, or walking along the Secret Lane, or being granted permission to go to the library all alone.

When I grew up and decided that I wanted to be a writer, I remembered how Maud Hart Lovelace had made small stories big. And I remembered that she had written about her childhood. Many of the incidents I have written about are small events from my own childhood—setting up a stand in our front yard to sell strawberries, wildflowers, and lemonade; putting on a carnival to raise money for the Red Cross; going on school field trips. The trick is making those small stories big enough—interesting or funny enough—to merit their places in books. I also found myself creating mostly girl characters—independent girls who operate not quite outside the world of adults, but not quite within it either. They hover somewhere between, with their own plans and big ideas, and friends to help carry them out.

Very much like Betsy, Tacy, and Tib.

—Ann M. Martin

Betsy-Tacy and Tib

Three can make the planets sing

—MARY CAROLYN DAVIES

1

Begging at Mrs. Ekstrom's

ETSY AND Tacy and Tib were three little girls who were friends. They never quarreled. Betsy and Tacy were friends first. They were good friends, and they never quarreled. When Tib moved into that neighborhood, and the three of them started playing together, grown-up people said:

"It's too bad! Betsy Ray and Tacy Kelly always played so nicely. Two little girls often do play nicely, but just let a third one come around. . . ." And they stopped, and their silence sounded as though they were saying: "then the trouble begins!"

But although so many people expected it, no trouble began with Betsy, Tacy and Tib. The three of them didn't quarrel, any more than the two of them had. They sometimes quarreled with Julia and Katie, though. Julia and Katie were Betsy's and Tacy's big sisters; they were bossy; and Betsy and Tacy and Tib didn't like to be bossed.

Betsy and Tacy lived on Hill Street, which ran straight up into a green hill and stopped. The small yellow cottage where the Ray family lived was the last house on that side of the street, and the rambling white house opposite where the Kelly family lived was the last house on that side. These two houses ended the street, and after that came the hill.

Tib didn't live on Hill Street. She lived on Pleasant Street. To get to Tib's house from the place where Betsy and Tacy lived you went one block down and one block over. (The second block was through a vacant lot.) Tib lived in a chocolate-colored house which was the most beautiful house Betsy and Tacy had ever been in. It had front stairs and back stairs and a tower and panes of colored glass in the front door.

Tib was the same age as Betsy and Tacy. They

were all eight years old. They were six when Tib came to live in Deep Valley, and now they were eight. Tacy was the tallest. She had long red ringlets and freckles and thin legs. Until she got acquainted with people Tacy was bashful. Tib was the smallest. She was little and dainty with round blue eyes and a fluff of yellow hair. She looked like a picture-book fairy, except, of course, that she didn't have wings. Betsy was the middle-sized one. She had plump legs and short brown braids which stuck out behind her ears. Her smile showed teeth which were parted in the middle, and Betsy was almost always smiling.

When Betsy ran out of doors in the morning, she came with a beam on her face. That was because it was fun to plan what she and Tacy and Tib were going to do. Betsy loved to think up things to do and Tacy and Tib loved to do them.

One morning Betsy ran out of her house and met Tacy who had just run out of hers. They met in the middle of the road and ran up to the bench which stood at the end of Hill Street. From that bench they could look 'way down the street. They often waited there for Tib.

Betsy and Tacy had to wait for Tib because they got ready to play sooner than she did. Betsy's mother was slim and quick; she didn't need much help around the house. And Tacy's mother had ten children besides Tacy, so of course there wasn't much for Tacy to do. Tib's mother had a hired girl to help her, but just the same Tib had to work. Tib's mother believed in children knowing how to work. Tib dusted the legs of the chairs and polished the silver. She was learning to cook and to sew.

Betsy and Tacy didn't mind waiting today. It was June, and the world smelled of roses. The sunshine was like powdered gold over the grassy hillside.

"What shall we do today?" asked Tacy.

"Let's go up on the Big Hill," Betsy answered.

The Big Hill wasn't the hill which ended Hill Street. That was the Hill Street Hill. The Big Hill rose up behind Betsy's house. And a white house stood at the top.

"Shall we take a picnic?" asked Tacy.

"I wish we could," said Betsy. "But it's pretty soon after breakfast to ask for a picnic."

"If I went in the house to ask," said Tacy, "I might have to help with the dishes."

"Better not go," said Betsy. "But we'll be hungry by the time we get to the top." She thought for a moment. "We may have to pretend we're beggars."

"What do you mean by that?" asked Tacy, her blue eyes beginning to sparkle.

"Why, muss up our hair and dirty our clothes and ask for something to eat at the white house."

"Oh! Oh!" cried Tacy. It was all she could say.

Just then Tib ran up. She looked so clean in a starched pink chambray dress that Betsy thought perhaps they had better not be beggars.

"What are we going to do?" asked Tib.

"We're going up on the Big Hill," said Betsy. "Of course, we have to ask."

They were eight years old, but they still couldn't climb the Big Hill without permission; Betsy and Tacy couldn't; Tib's mother always told her that she could go wherever Betsy and Tacy were allowed to go. Tib's house was too far away to run to every time they had to ask permission.

Betsy and Tacy sent Paul, who was Tacy's little brother, into their houses to ask permission now. Paul trotted into Tacy's house and into Betsy's house, and he trotted back with word that they could go. So Betsy and Tacy and Tib started walking up the Big Hill.

Julia was practising her music lesson, and the sound of the scales she was playing flashed out of the house as they passed. It sounded as though Julia were enjoying herself.

"I wouldn't like to be playing the piano today," said Betsy.

"Neither would I," said Tacy.

"Neither would I," said Tib. "Of course," she

added, "we don't know how."

Neither Betsy nor Tacy would have pointed that out. Tib was always pointing such things out. But Betsy and Tacy liked her just the same.

"We could learn quick enough if we wanted to," said Betsy. "I can play chopsticks now."

They came to a ridge where wild roses were in bloom. They stopped to smell them. They passed a thorn apple tree where they would pick thorn apples later. Now the tree was covered with little hard green balls. There were lots of trees on that side of the road and the grass was deep and full of flowers. On the other side was a fenced-in pasture with Mr. Williams' cow in it.

At last they came to the top of the hill. They could look down now on the roofs of Hill Street. They could see the school house where they all went to school and the chocolate-colored house where Tib lived. They could see all over the town of Deep Valley, 'way to the Big Mill. And deep in the valley they could see a silver ribbon. That was the river.

The top of the hill was flat, and there were oak trees scattered about. The white house stood in the middle. It was a small house with a flower garden at the front. Some people named Ekstrom lived there. Behind the Ekstroms' house was a ravine, with a spring of water in it, and a brook. Betsy and

Tacy and Tib had been down in the ravine, but not without Julia and Katie.

"Let's go down in the ravine," said Betsy.

They took hold of hands.

The way to the ravine was through the Ekstroms' back yard. Betsy and Tacy and Tib didn't know the Ekstroms, but they had seen them often going up and down the hill. They didn't see any of the Ekstroms now. They saw a dog who barked at them in a friendly sort of way. They saw some hens who clucked sociably. And through an open barn door they saw a cow. They went past the kitchen garden and came to the edge of the ravine.

A steep twisting path led into the ravine. The hillside was crowded with trees. There were big trees and seedling trees, old graying trees and fresh fine green ones. The grass was full of red and yellow columbine.

Betsy and Tacy and Tib descended carefully, picking flowers as they went.

All the way down they could hear the brook, and when they reached the bottom they could see it, rushing over its stones. There was a spring with four boards around it. When you leaned over to drink, the water smacked your face. They drank from the spring and the water tasted good, but it wasn't as good as something to eat would have been.

"I'm hungry," said Tacy.

"So am I," said Tib.

"Let's suck the honey from our columbine," said Betsy, so they sucked the honey out of all their flowers. But they were still hungry.

Betsy looked around.

"There's syrup in those maple trees," she said. "If we'd brought a knife, we could cut a hole and get some."

"And make a fire and fry pancakes!" cried Tacy. She and Betsy jumped up to hunt for a knife, but Tib stopped them.

"You need flour to make pancakes," Tib said. Tib knew. She could cook.

"Well I'm hungry," said Tacy. "I wonder where we're going to get something to eat." And she looked at Betsy hard.

Betsy knew she was thinking of what Betsy had said about begging, and she almost wished she hadn't said it, but she was getting hungrier every minute. She spoke loudly and importantly.

"We *may* have to beg," she said.

"What's that?" asked Tib.

"Muss up our hair and dirty our dresses and pretend we need something to eat."

"We *do* need something to eat," said Tacy. "No pretend about it."

"My mother wouldn't like me to muss up my dress," said Tib. She meant that her mother wouldn't *like* her to muss up her dress. She didn't mean she wouldn't do it.

"She'd rather have you muss up your dress than starve," said Betsy. "We might starve to death down in this ravine."

"Might we?" asked Tib.

"I feel sort of starved already," said Betsy.

"So do I," said Tacy. "I feel weak."

They listened to the spring bubbling out of the ground.

"If we *all* got mussed up," said Betsy, "maybe our mothers would see that it couldn't be helped." So they began to muss each other up.

It was fun mussing each other up. It was such fun that they almost forgot they were hungry. They loosened Betsy's braids and tangled Tacy's ringlets and ruffled Tib's fluffy hair until she looked like a dandelion gone to seed. Then they put mud on one another. Mud on cheeks and noses, and mud on arms and legs. There was plenty of mud beside the brook and they put on plenty. They put it on their dresses and smooched it down with their hands.

When they had finished they began to climb out of the ravine.

"Who's going to ask for something to eat?" asked Tacy.

"Tib," said Betsy firmly. "Because she's the littlest. But you and I will stand right beside her, so we'll be just as much to blame as she is."

"That's right," said Tib.

They had reached the Ekstroms' kitchen garden, and when the dog saw them he began to bark. He barked differently now from the way he had barked when they went down. He barked as though he didn't like the way they looked.

They went past the henhouse, and the hens clucked. They went past the barn, and the cow mooed. They went up to the back door, and the dog barked harder than ever. He yelped and snapped.

The door was open. Only the screen door was closed to keep out flies. There were strips of paper hanging down it, to flutter and scare flies when the door was opened. Between those strips of paper they could see a woman in the kitchen. Betsy knocked.

Mrs. Ekstrom came to the door. She was small and thin. She had yellow hair pulled into a knob and a thin tired face. She looked at Betsy and Tacy and Tib and said, "Heavens and earth!" Then she said, "What happened? What's the matter?" And she looked at Betsy hard. "You're the little Ray girl," she said.

"We're hungry," said Tib.

"And the little Kelly girl," Mrs. Ekstrom continued, staring now at Tacy.

"We're hungry," said Tib.

"And the little Muller girl, I think. *Aren't* you the little Muller girl?" she asked addressing Tib.

"We're hungry," said Tib.

"Hungry!" said Mrs. Ekstrom. "You're lots besides hungry. What happened to you anyway?"

"We got hungry," said Tib.

Betsy and Tacy didn't say a word, but they tried to act as hungry as they could. Betsy put her hands over her stomach and leaned forward and groaned. Tacy forgot to be bashful and she opened and shut her mouth. She opened and shut her mouth and made queer hungry noises.

Mrs. Ekstrom's face broke into a smile.

She opened the kitchen door to let them come in, and gave them a paper to stand on.

They had come to a good house to be hungry in, Betsy saw at once. Mrs. Ekstrom was baking cookies. They had just come out of the oven, and they smelled delicious. They were sugar cookies. Betsy and Tacy and Tib watched Mrs. Ekstrom while she lifted cookies on a pancake turner and filled a plate.

She put the plateful of cookies down on the table.

"Wait while I get some milk," she said, and she

went into the pantry.

Betsy and Tacy and Tib looked at the cookies. They looked good.

While Mrs. Ekstrom was in the pantry, the dog started to bark. His bark didn't sound angry any more. It was just the friendly sociable kind of bark he had barked when they first went through the dooryard. Steps sounded outside and someone knocked on the kitchen door. Mrs. Ekstrom darted out of the pantry.

"How do you do, Mrs. Ekstrom?" came a voice. It was Julia's voice, sounding very grown-up; and Julia could sound extremely grown-up although she was not yet eleven. "Have you seen Betsy and Tacy and Tib, Mrs. Ekstrom?" Julia asked.

"We're looking for them," Katie's voice added.

Betsy stopped rubbing her stomach, and Tacy shut her mouth. Tib turned her round blue eyes from one to the other for instructions, and Betsy said, "Run!"

There was an open door in the kitchen which led to the front hall. Betsy and Tacy and Tib ran down the hall and out to the porch and jumped three steps into the flower garden. They ran and they ran and they ran, and they ran down the Big Hill.

They ran fast for they thought they heard Julia and Katie behind them. But they were mistaken. It was their own feet they had heard. When they got to the bottom of the hill, Julia and Katie weren't there at all. They weren't even in sight.

"They're up there eating our cookies!" said Betsy.

"They make me mad!" said Tacy.

"They make me mad too!" said Tib.

The three of them sat down to rest, breathless and panting, their legs stuck out before them.

Betsy looked at her mud-streaked legs, and after a moment she began to smile.

"But we were the ones who almost starved," she said. "We were the ones who put mud on ourselves and went begging."

"We had all the fun," said Tacy. "We always do."

"I'd have liked a cookie, though," Tib said matter-of-factly. Tib always said things like that. But Betsy and Tacy liked her just the same.

2

Learning to Fly

ETSY AND Tacy and Tib were scolded for going begging. They weren't surprised that they were scolded, but they were surprised at what they were scolded for. They had expected to be scolded for putting mud on themselves, for mussing up their dresses and tangling their hair. But none of the fathers and mothers seemed to mind that very much. What they minded was their asking for something to eat.

The fathers and mothers tried to explain. It was telling a lie to pretend that they were hungry when they weren't.

"But we were!" cried Betsy and Tacy and Tib.

"Well, even if you were, it was wrong to ask food from Mrs. Ekstrom when you had plenty at home."

"You ought to respect yourselves too much," said Betsy's father, "to ask for help you don't need."

Betsy and Tacy and Tib tried to understand.

They understood that they had been naughty. They understood that they weren't to go begging again. For besides being scolded they were punished. They were forbidden to go up on the Big Hill for a month.

They had never wanted so much to go up on the Big Hill as that month when they weren't allowed to go. From Betsy's backyard maple it looked tall and full of mystery. Julia and Katie went up and came down with their arms full of flowers ... wild sweet peas and Queen Anne's lace and white and yellow daisies.

Betsy and Tacy took care of Betsy's baby sister, Margaret. And Tib took care of her baby brother, Hobbie; Hobson was his name. Their mothers thought it was a good thing for them to make themselves useful. Besides, they couldn't think of anything else to do.

It was strange . . . when they were allowed to go up on the Big Hill they didn't go often. Almost all their games were played down on Hill Street or up on the Hill Street Hill. Yet now that they weren't allowed to climb the Big Hill they couldn't think of anything else worth doing.

But one day Betsy had an idea.

It was a warm afternoon, and they were sitting under the backyard maple. They were taking care of Hobbie and Margaret, of course. Hobbie was in his carriage, and Margaret was staggering around through the grass the way a two-year-old does. Tacy's little brother Paul was there too. He was playing with a cart. Paul was always playing with carts.

The world was so quiet, you could hear the bees buzzing over Betsy's mother's nasturtiums. The air was full of a nasturtium smell which matched their red and orange colors. Betsy stared up into the backyard maple, and Tib jiggled Hobbie's carriage (hoping he would fall asleep), and Tacy chewed a piece of grass and kept her eyes on Margaret, who wasn't supposed to go too near the terrace for fear of tumbling down.

"There ought to be *some*thing we can do," said Betsy, staring into the tree.

"Well, what is it, I'd like to know?" asked Tacy, jumping up to pull Margaret back from the terrace.

"It will have to be something with babies in it," said Tib, jiggling the carriage.

Betsy watched a bluebird take off from the maple on a voyage through the sunlit air.

"What *can* we do?" she murmured, watching him; and just as the bluebird melted into the sky, somewhere above Tacy's roof, she sat up with very bright eyes.

"I know!" she said. "We'll learn to fly."

"To fly!" cried Tacy and Tib.

"To fly!" answered Betsy positively. "Birds can fly. Why can't we? We're just as smart as birds." Tacy and Tib didn't answer, and Betsy went on: "Smarter! Did you ever hear of birds going into the Third Grade the way we're going to do this fall? We can fly just as well as the birds, only we have to learn how, of course. And that's what we're going to do right now."

"How?" asked Tacy.

"We'll start jumping off things. First we'll jump off something low. And then something higher. And then something lots higher. And so on. We'll jump off the house at last, but we prob'ly won't get to that today."

"What will we use for wings?" asked Tib.

"Our arms," said Betsy. "We'll wave them like this." And she began to run and wave her arms, and

Tacy and Tib ran after her and waved their arms too, and Paul stopped playing with his cart and ran and waved his arms.

"No, Paul," said Betsy. "You're too young to fly. It's dangerous. But you can watch us, and so can Margaret and Hobbie."

So Paul sat down in the grass and watched, and they put Margaret into her gocart and she watched too. Hobbie had fallen asleep.

"We'll begin with our hitching block," said Betsy, and she ran out to the hitching block and jumped off, waving her arms. "It's easy!" she cried.

"I'll go next," said Tacy, and she jumped off, waving her arms. She waved them beautifully.

Tib went last. She went as lightly as a puff of wind, but she called out, "I'm afraid I only jumped."

"Jumping and flying are a good deal the same, just at first," Betsy explained.

Next they tried the porch railing. And again Betsy went off first. She waved her arms, but she landed on the ground with a pretty hard thump. "It takes time to learn, of course," she said, rubbing her feet.

Tacy went next, and she didn't fly quite so nicely this time. Her waving wasn't so good.

Tib stood on the railing and smiled before she flew. Tib had had dancing lessons, and besides she was light as a feather. She waved her arms as she came down

and she landed on the tips of her toes.

"Tib," said Betsy, "you're learning how to fly just fine. I think you'll be the first one of us to learn."

"It feels just like jumping," answered Tib.

"Well, it isn't," said Betsy. "It's beginning to be flying. Next we'll try the backyard maple."

Now the backyard maple was a very big tree. Of course they could climb it; they were all good tree climbers. But the lowest branch was a long way from the ground.

"It's pretty high to jump from," Tacy pointed out.

"It isn't as high as the house will be," said Betsy. "We'll be flying off the house tomorrow, prob'ly."

"I'll go first," said Tib, "because I fly the best."

"All right," said Betsy and Tacy.

Tib went up the tree in a flash. She climbed out on the lowest branch, but there wasn't room to stand up; she had to squat. She waved her arms, though, and kept her balance too.

"What kind of a bird am I?" she called, waving her arms.

"You're a Tibbin," answered Betsy. "You're a Tibbin bird."

"Here comes the Tibbin!" cried Tib, and she waved her arms and came down. She fell on her knees, but she laughed as she dusted them off. "I like this flying game, Betsy," she said.

"I'll go next," said Tacy, because Betsy didn't say a word about going next. "That is, if Paul is all right. Are you all right, Paul?"

Paul said he was all right.

"Of course I'm sort of looking after Paul," said Tacy. "But I'll go next, unless you want to, Betsy."

"Oh, you can go next if you want to," said Betsy.

So Tacy went next.

She climbed out on the lowest branch. But she sat on it; she didn't squat. She didn't even try to wave.

"What kind of a bird am I?" she asked. But you could see it was only to pass the time. She didn't look happy as Tib had looked; she looked scared.

"You're a Tacin," answered Betsy. "You're a Tacin bird."

"Oh," said Tacy.

She waited a long time before she flew, but at last she flew. She let herself down, holding tight to the branch with her hands; then she loosened her hold and dropped.

"That's good," Betsy said. "That's fine, Tacy. Well, I suppose it's my turn."

Nobody said it wasn't.

Betsy got to the lowest branch and sat on it. She held on tight and swung her legs. She didn't fly though.

"When are you going to fly?" asked Tib.

"In a minute," answered Betsy. She sat there and swung her legs.

"What kind of a bird are you, Betsy?" Tacy asked.

"I'm a Betsin," answered Betsy. "I'm a Betsin bird."

She looked up into the leafy world above her, and she looked down at the ground. The ground was a long way off.

"Don't Betsin birds like to fly?" asked Tib.

"Oh, yes," said Betsy. "They love to fly." But still she didn't fly. She looked up again into the cool green branches.

"They like to fly so well," she said at last, "that

it's a wonder they ever stopped doing it. But they did. Do you want to know why?"

"Why?" asked Tacy and Tib.

"Sit down and I'll tell you," said Betsy. "It's very interesting. Maybe Paul would like to hear too."

So Tacy and Tib sat down in the grass to listen. Paul put aside his cart and leaned against Tacy, and Tib jiggled Margaret's gocart. Hobbie was still asleep.

"Once upon a time," said Betsy, "there were three little birds named Tibbin, Tacin, and Betsin.

"There was something funny about these birds. They used to be little girls.

"They turned into birds one day when they were trying to learn to fly. It was only sort of a game at first, but they learned to fly just fine, and so they got turned into birds.

"Tib got turned first. She took dancing lessons and she learned to fly awfully quick. The real birds saw how pretty she flew and one of them . . . it was a bluebird . . . said, 'Mercy, that little girl flies so pretty she ought to be a bird.' So he turned her into a Tibbin. A Tibbin is yellow like a wild canary; and Tib had yellow curls.

"Tacy got turned next. She had long red ringlets so she got turned into a Tacin. That's red like a robin.

"Betsy got turned last. She got turned into a Betsin, because a Betsin is brown like a wren and

Betsy had brown hair.

"Betsin, Tacin and Tibbin just loved being birds. They had all kinds of fun. They made themselves a nest right here in the backyard maple, and they lived in it together. They found wild strawberries to eat, and Julia and Katie (they were Betsy's and Tacy's big sisters) put out cake crumbs for them. Julia and Katie never dreamed they were giving their cake crumbs to Betsy and Tacy and Tib. You put out cake crumbs too, Paul. You put out delicious crumbs.

"Betsin and Tacin and Tibbin flew in and out of the branches; those green branches up there. They flew up to the roofs of their houses and even up to the clouds. They liked the sunset clouds, and at sunset time they each used to pick out a cloud and sit on it. The Betsin bird took a pink cloud and the Tacin bird took a purple one and the Tibbin bird took a yellow one, most always.

"One night they were sitting on their sunset clouds and Betsin heard someone crying. She said to Tacin and Tibbin, 'Who's that I hear crying?' And Tacin and Tibbin said, 'We don't hear anything.' And Betsin said, 'Listen! Listen hard!' So they listened hard, and sure enough they heard somebody crying. 'We'd better fly down and find out who that is,' said Betsin. So they all flew down to Hill Street.

"And when they got there, they found out that it was their mothers crying. Their mothers were crying hard like this: 'Ooh! Ooh! Ooh!' 'Ooh! Ooh! Ooh!' 'Where are Betsy and Tacy and Tib?' 'Where are Betsy and Tacy and Tib?' So then Betsin and Tacin and Tibbin knew why their mothers were crying. They knew it was on account of them. And it made them feel funny."

Tacy interrupted.

"It makes me feel funny now," she said, and her voice sounded all choked up.

"It makes me feel funny too," said Tib, winking her eyes. "I never heard my mamma cry."

"Oh, their fathers were crying too," said Betsy. "At least they would have been crying if they hadn't been fathers. They were feeling awfully bad. And Julia and Katie were crying. Julia said, 'Boo! hoo! I'm sorry I used to be bossy to Betsy!' And Katie said, 'Boo! hoo! I'm sorry I used to be bossy to Tacy too.' And they cried, and they cried, and they cried . . ."

"And *I* cried!" cried Paul, interrupting. "I cried!" And no sooner had he said it than he began to cry in earnest. He put his curly head into Tacy's lap and wailed.

"But Paul!" cried Betsy. "It's going to come out all right."

Paul kept on crying.

And when Margaret heard Paul cry, she began to cry. She had been almost asleep with all Tib's jiggling, but now she woke up and began to cry. And Hobbie woke up and began to cry too. But Paul cried hardest of all.

"Stop, Paul!" cried Betsy from the maple. "Hear how it's going to come out!"

Paul lifted a streaming face and sniffed.

"Betsin and Tacin and Tibbin felt bad just the way you do."

"Did they?" asked Paul, sniffing.

"Certainly they did. They didn't want to keep on being birds after they knew how everybody felt. And Betsin said, 'I don't believe we'd better be birds any more. We've had lots of fun being birds, but I think it's time we stopped.' And Tacin and Tibbin said that was exactly how they felt. So Tibbin changed herself out of a bird, and she climbed down the maple. And Tacin changed *her*self out of a bird, and *she* climbed down the maple. And Betsin changed *her*self out of a bird, and *she* climbed down the maple. Like this," said Betsy.

And she climbed down the maple.

Just then Betsy's mother came out the kitchen door with some gingerbread. Paul had stopped crying, but Margaret and Hobbie were still crying hard, and Betsy's mother thought that perhaps some gingerbread would help. So she brought out enough for everybody.

Julia and Katie came down from the Big Hill and they had some too. Then Julia went into the house to practise her music lesson and Katie took Paul home to wash him up for supper. Mrs. Ray had already taken Margaret in, and Tib thought that perhaps she had better wheel Hobbie home.

Betsy and Tacy walked a piece with her. They always did. They always walked as far as the middle of the vacant lot. They were talking as they walked, about what they would do up on the Big Hill after they were allowed to go up there again. All of a sudden Tib interrupted.

"Betsy," she said. "I know a joke on you."

"Do you?" asked Betsy.

"You didn't ever fly down out of the maple."

"*Didn't* I?" asked Betsy, sounding surprised.

"No," said Tib. "You didn't. I did. And Tacy did. But you got to telling that story and forgot all about it. It's a joke on you," said Tib, laughing.

Betsy looked at Tacy but Tacy was looking the other way. She was looking the other way hard.

"Oh," said Betsy. "Well here's the middle of the vacant lot. We'll see you in the morning."

3

The Flying Lady

STRANGELY ENOUGH, soon after they tried
to learn to fly, Betsy and Tacy and Tib saw a
Flying Lady. It happened this way:

A Street Fair came to Deep Valley. A carnival,
some people called it. It was a little like a circus, but
it lasted for a week. And instead of being held out
on the circus ground, it was held on Front Street.

Front Street was decorated with bunting and flags. There were tents and booths at every corner. The air was filled with excitement from the music of the merry-go-round and the voices of men who shouted in front of the tents, urging people to come in.

There were plenty of people to go into all the tents, for the sidewalks were crowded. Men and women and children walked up and down, up and down Front Street, buying whips and balloons and lemonade and popcorn and peanuts and ice cream. There were open booths where you could shoot at dolls, and if you hit a doll you won it. Tacy's brother George won a doll, and he gave it to Tacy.

Betsy and Tacy and Tib went to the Street Fair with their fathers and mothers. They rode on the merry-go-round and they rode on the Ferris Wheel, rising high into the quiet air above the dust and glitter. The Street Fair was full of wonders, but one surpassed all others, and that was the Flying Lady.

Mrs. Muller invited Betsy and Tacy to go with Tib to see the Flying Lady. It was fun to go to the Street Fair all together. They wore their best dimity dresses, trimmed with lace and insertion, and their best summer hats with flowers and ribbons on them. Mrs. Muller looked nice too. She wore a shirt waist and skirt and a round straw hat. She bought each one a bag of popcorn; it was hot and buttery.

Before they went into the show they stood in front of the tent eating popcorn and listening to the man on the platform.

"Right this way!" he shouted through a megaphone, pacing up and down, dripping sweat. "Right this way to the one and only Flying Lady! She's beautiful! She's marvelous! She flies! Come right in and see for yourself, folks! It's the wonder of two continents. It's the thrill of a lifetime! And all for one dime . . . two small nickels!"

Betsy touched Mrs. Muller's sleeve.

"Is it time to go in, Mrs. Muller?"

"Not yet," Mrs. Muller answered.

"Right this way," the man kept on shouting, "to the one and only Flying Lady. She's beautiful! She's marvelous! She flies! The show's beginning, folks. Step right up and get your tickets. You can't afford to miss a moment of this beautiful, educational, inspiring, astounding, spectacular exhibition. . . ."

Tacy poked Betsy, and Betsy looked at Mrs. Muller sideways. She hated to ask again. But she knew Tacy was worried, and she was worried too. Maybe Mrs. Muller wasn't listening? Maybe she hadn't heard what the man had said about the show beginning?

"Do you s'pose we ought to go in, Mrs. Muller?" she asked.

"There's plenty of time," Mrs. Muller answered.

The man was pacing up and down now like a lion in a cage.

"Right this way," he shouted, "to the one and only Flying Lady! She's beautiful! She's marvelous! She flies! Don't run, folks! But hurry just a little! Hurry just a————"

Tacy poked Betsy again, a hard jab this time. Betsy knew it wouldn't be polite to keep on asking Mrs. Muller to go in, so she poked Tib, as a hint that Tib might ask her. Tib said right out loud, "What do you want, Betsy? What are you poking me for?" That was just like Tib. Fortunately Mrs. Muller was ready to go in anyway. She said, "Well, come along, children!"

She bought the tickets from a lady with golden hair. The lady had three golden teeth too; they were right in front, and they showed when she smiled. She smiled at them all, but especially at Tib, and she said to Mrs. Muller, "She looks as though she could fly herself." At that Tacy poked Betsy, and Betsy poked Tib, and this time Tib understood what the poke meant, and they all began to laugh.

There were plenty of seats empty. In fact there were only three or four seats filled. But Betsy and Tacy didn't mind that. It was fun to be able to choose the seats they wanted. They tried seats in the back of the tent, and they tried seats in the middle, and they tried seats in the very front row.

"We ought to sit close," Betsy whispered, "because we're trying to learn to fly ourselves. We ought to see how she does it."

"That's right," said Tacy. And Tib thought so too. So they sat down in the very front row.

The tent was darker than most tents. There were heavy curtains hung all around to make it extra dark. And of course there were curtains concealing the stage. They looked like black velvet.

Out in front the man was still shouting: "She's beautiful! She's marvelous! She flies!" Sometimes he said that the show was just beginning. But it didn't begin. More people came in though; and more, and more.

Betsy and Tacy and Tib finished their popcorn and wiped their fingers on the handkerchiefs which their mothers had pinned to their dresses. They looked around until they had seen everything there was to see. Still the show didn't begin.

"When do you think it will begin, Mamma?" asked Tib.

"Pretty soon," Mrs. Muller answered.

And pretty soon it did.

It began with music which came from behind the curtains. And the music changed everything. It brought magic into the dark tent. The piece being played was a piece Julia played. It was named *Narcissus*.

"Dee, *dee*, dee, *dee*, dee dee dee dee dee dee *dee*."

Betsy and Tacy and Tib took hold of hands.

The curtains concealing the stage were drawn aside, but the stage was as dark as a cave. It was hung with black draperies, and the music made things mysterious.

"Dee, *dee*, dee, *dee*, dee dee dee dee dee dee *dee*."

Just as Julia played it.

"Dee, *dee*

"Dee, *dee*. . . ."

And then something white appeared, parting the black draperies which mistily filled the stage. The something white was rising slowly up. Wings (or arms) were waving in time to the music.

Betsy and Tacy and Tib leaned forward, staring. Their eyes grew accustomed to the darkness, and they saw that the floating figure was indeed that of a lady. She was dressed in white robes which covered her arms (or wings). Red ringlets like Tacy's hung down across her shoulders. A bright light shone on her face, but the rest of her was in shadow.

"Dee, *dee*, dee, *dee*, dee dee dee dee dee dee *dee*."

She smiled at the people as she flew.

"Dee, *dee*, dee, *dee*, dee dee dee dee dee dee *dee*."

Up and down she went, in time to the music.

And not only up and down, but from side to side of the stage. Betsy squeezed Tacy's hands, and Tib's, and Tacy and Tib squeezed back. Their eyes strained through the darkness in order not to miss a movement of the glowing airy figure flying up and down, back and across, to that tune which Julia could play.

They could have watched for hours, but the show did not last very long. In no time at all the curtains were drawn, the music had stopped, and people were clapping their hands and pushing out of the tent. Mrs. Muller, with Betsy, Tacy and Tib, came out last of all.

"Did you like it?" Mrs. Muller asked.

"Oh, yes!" said Betsy and Tacy and Tib. At first that was all they could say.

Mrs. Muller took them across the street to Heinz's Restaurant, and each one had a dish of ice cream. It was vanilla ice cream, and they had vanilla wafers with it. They talked about the Flying Lady as they ate.

"She looked like Tacy, Mamma," Tib said.

"Yes, she did," said Mrs. Muller.

That made Tacy bashful.

"I wish it hadn't been quite so dark," Betsy said.

"I think they made it dark on purpose," Mrs. Muller answered, smiling.

"I wish they hadn't," Betsy said. But she didn't say why.

Of course the reason was that if it hadn't been so dark she and Tacy and Tib could have learned more about flying. Tacy and Tib were thinking the very same thing. But they didn't discuss that with Mrs. Muller. They doubted that a grown-up would understand.

They told Mrs. Muller that they had had a nice time, and she took Betsy to her father's shoe store and Tacy to the office where her father sold sewing machines. Betsy and Tacy and Tib all rode home with their fathers, and they didn't have a chance to discuss the show with each other, until after supper. Then they met on the bench at the top of Hill Street.

They had changed out of their best dresses and taken off their shoes and stockings. It was pleasant to sit with their feet in the dewy grass and talk about the Flying Lady.

"If we look hard," said Betsy, "maybe we'll see her flying through the sky."

"I'll bet we will," said Tacy. "If I could fly, I wouldn't fly just in a dark old tent."

"Neither would I," said Tib. "I'd go up in the sky and do tricks."

They looked all over the sky, but they didn't see a sign of her. There were no white draperies floating among the pink clouds in the west.

"That's funny," said Betsy, "for a sunset would be such fun to fly in."

The Flying Lady did not come, and the sunset faded. It was almost time to go home when they noticed color in the northern sky, far down over the town. Faint music drifted from the same direction. They knew that it came from the Street Fair.

"My papa and mamma are going there tonight," Tib said. "My mamma wants my papa to see the Flying Lady."

Betsy and Tacy looked at each other in sudden understanding. They spoke almost at once.

"Of course!" cried Betsy.

"She's down there making money!" cried Tacy.

"She couldn't be flying up here on the hill," they explained to Tib, "when she's flying down there in the tent."

"That's right," said Tib. "Well, maybe she'll fly in the sky tomorrow morning."

"Let's come up here early to look," Betsy said.

And they all ran home.

Betsy and Tacy met on the bench right after breakfast and started looking for the Flying Lady. It was a sunshiny sweet-smelling morning, just the kind of a day it would be fun to fly in. The sky was full of little fat chunks of cloud.

"Marshmallows probably," said Betsy, "in case she gets hungry."

"Or cushions in case she gets tired," said Tacy.

They stared faithfully upward.

They were staring upward so hard that they didn't see Tib until she called out to them. Then they looked and saw her running up the street. As soon as they saw her, they saw that something was wrong. And sure enough, as she sat down, she said:

"I know something terrible."

"What is it?" Betsy asked.

"That Flying Lady," said Tib, "she doesn't really fly."

"I don't believe it," said Tacy.

"My papa said so," said Tib. "He was explaining it at breakfast."

And Tib explained it to them.

The lady was sitting on one end of an iron bar, she said. The bar was like a see-saw. The lady sat on one end and something heavy sat on the other and moved her up and down, over and across.

"That's why they kept the tent so dark," Tib said. "So we couldn't see the see-saw."

There was a moment's stricken silence.

But then Betsy jumped up and began to jump up and down.

"That gives me an idea!" she cried.

"A show!" cried Tacy, reading her mind.

"In our buggy shed!" cried Betsy. "We'll ask my papa to wheel the surrey out, and we'll cover the window with a gunny sack, to make the buggy shed as dark as that tent was. And we'll put a see-saw inside . . ."

"I know where there's a lovely plank," Tacy interrupted.

"We'll have a curtain across the middle," Betsy hurried on. "And we'll put out chunks of wood for seats. And we'll ask admission, five pins admission and a penny for the grown-ups. Julia could play *Narcissus*, but the piano's too far away."

"We could hum it," Tacy said.

But Tib had a better plan than that.

"Tom can play it on his violin," she said.

They knew a little boy named Tom who could play the violin. He could play *Narcissus*.

"Yes, Tom can play his violin," said Betsy. "And I'll stand out in front and shout for people to come. 'Right this way to the one and only Flying Lady! She's beautiful! She's marvelous! She flies!'"

"What will I do?" asked Tib.

"You'll sell tickets," said Betsy. "We'll paste a strip of gold paper over your front teeth."

"Who'll be the Flying Lady?" Tacy asked nervously.

"You," said Betsy. "Because you look just like her. Do you s'pose you can wear one of your sister Mary's night gowns? After I get through calling out about the show, and Tib gets through selling tickets, we'll go inside behind the curtain. We'll sit on the back end of the see-saw, to make you go up and down."

Tacy didn't like the idea any too well.

But that was what they did, that very day. They gave a Flying Lady show in Betsy's father's buggy shed. All the children of Hill Street came, and a few grown-ups. Mrs. Benson, who didn't have any children of her own, came and paid a nickel.

And Betsy shouted out in front, "Right this way to the one and only Flying Lady. She's beautiful! She's marvelous! She flies." And Tib took tickets, showing her gold teeth all she could. And the little boy named Tom played *Narcissus* on his violin. He played it beautifully.

They gave a wonderful show but there was one unfortunate incident. Betsy and Tib made Tacy's

end of the see-saw go so high that Tacy got scared. She clutched the plank and cried, "Stop! Stop! I'm falling!" And of course a few rude children laughed, but most of them applauded.

After that show Betsy and Tacy and Tib stopped trying to fly. They never tried to fly again.

4
The House in Tib's Basement

BETSY, TACY and Tib didn't always play on Hill Street. Sometimes they played at Tib's house, over on Pleasant Street.

They loved to play at Tib's house for they thought it very beautiful with its chocolate color and its tower and the panes of colored glass in the front door.

They loved especially to play in Tib's basement.

At Betsy's house there wasn't any basement. There was only a cellar. Her father opened a trap door in the kitchen and took a stub of candle and went down and came back with apples which were kept there in a barrel, or perhaps a jug of cider. At Tacy's house it was much the same. But at Tib's house there was a basement.

It was floored with cement, and it was warm and dry and sunny. In the center was a strange contrivance called a furnace, which heated Tib's house. This was the only furnace in Deep Valley. In the basement also there were tubs for washing clothes. There were closets where glass jars full of pickles and jellies were stored. And there was a great open space where wood was piled, stacked in long orderly rows.

One day just before school began Betsy and Tacy came over to play with Tib. They wiped their feet hard on the mat at Tib's back door, for Tib's house was very clean. After they had wiped their feet hard, they rapped and the hired girl came to the door.

"Hello," said Betsy. "We came over to play with Tib."

"Hello," said the hired girl. Her name was Matilda. She was old and wore glasses and had graying yellow braids wound round and round her head. "Have you wiped your feet?" she asked, looking down at their shoes.

"Yes, we have," said Betsy.

"Well, it doesn't matter anyway," said Matilda, "for Tib is down in the basement. And there's such a mess there; it couldn't be worse."

"What kind of a mess?" Betsy asked eagerly, and Tacy's blue eyes began to dance. A mess! That sounded like fun.

"Go see for yourselves," said Matilda. "You can go down the outside way."

The two sloping doors which admitted from the outside of the house to the basement were flung open. Betsy and Tacy scampered down the stairs. And down in the basement they did indeed find a mess. A beautiful mess!

The winter's supply of wood had been thrown into the basement but it had not yet been piled; it had just been thrown in helter skelter. There seemed to be an ocean of wood, and rising like islands were two small yellow heads, belonging to Tib and her little brother Freddie.

Tib had two brothers, but the one named Hobbie was hardly more than a baby. Frederick was Paul's age; he was old enough to play with; and like Tib he was good natured and easy to play with.

"We're building a house out of wood," he shouted now, as Betsy and Tacy waded joyfully in.

"Come on and help!" cried Tib.

Betsy and Tacy took off their hats and helped.

They piled the wood just the way Tib and Freddie told them to. For Tib and Freddie were good at building houses; their father was an architect. This house they were building was like a real house. It was wonderful.

It was big enough to sit down in. It was even big enough to stand up in, if you didn't stand too straight. It had a window, and a doorway you could walk through, if you stooped only a little.

They found some boards and laid them across the top for a roof.

"Now it can't rain in," Betsy said.

They worked so hard that they grew warm and sticky and dirty and very tired. But it was such fun that they were amazed when they heard the whistles blowing for twelve o'clock.

"Oh, dear, we must go home for dinner," Betsy said. "But we'll hurry back."

"We'll eat fast," Tacy said.

"We'll eat fast too," said Tib, and she and Freddie hurried up the stairs.

Betsy and Tacy ran all the way home to their dinners.

"Mercy goodness, what's the matter?" asked Betsy's mother when Betsy ran into the house. "Your cheeks are like fire."

"Oh, Mamma!" cried Betsy. "We're having such fun. We're building a house in Tib's basement."

"When can we move in?" asked Betsy's father, who was already eating his dinner with Margaret in the high chair beside him. Betsy's father loved to joke.

Betsy washed her hands and face and sat down opposite Julia. She thought she ate her dinner quicker than a wink but she wasn't quite through when she heard Tacy yoo-hooing from her hitching block. Tacy's mother wouldn't let her come over to the Rays' house when they were eating a meal. She didn't think it was polite. So Tacy always waited on the hitching block. But she yoo-hooed once in a while.

Betsy gobbled her peach pie and gulped her milk. "It's Julia's turn to wipe the dishes. 'xcuse me?" she asked, jumping up.

Her braids flew out behind her as she vanished through the door. She and Tacy took hold of hands and ran down Hill Street.

As fast as they had been, Tib and Freddie were in the basement before them.

"We have to hurry," Tib explained, "for a man is coming at four o'clock to pile this wood."

"And we won't have a house any more," Freddie said, as though he didn't like it.

"It's a long time 'til four o'clock," Betsy said.

"Where'd you get the carpet?" Tacy asked.

"Our mamma gave it to us," Tib and Freddie answered proudly.

It was a beautiful carpet. It was red with yellow roses in it. They spread it down inside their house and placed chunks of wood for chairs.

When they had finished they sat down inside their house. There was room for all, although it was crowded. Tib didn't mind if Freddie put his feet in her lap. Betsy and Tacy didn't mind being squeezed against each other.

"Has your funny paper come?" Betsy asked.

Tib's father's paper came all the way from Milwaukee. There was a Sunday edition, and that had a funny paper in it.

"Yes, it came today," said Tib, and she ran up-stairs to get it.

They squeezed into their little house again, and Betsy read the funny paper out loud, all about Buster Brown and Alphonse and Gaston and the Katzenjammer Kids. Matilda came down to visit them, bringing some coffee cake. (Butter and sugar and cinnamon were pleasantly mixed on the top.)

It was fun to eat coffee cake and read the funny paper in their own crowded little house.

"I wish it would never get to be four o'clock," said Freddie. Betsy and Tacy and Tib wished so too.

But bye and bye it got to be four o'clock.

A strange man came down the stairs in his shirt sleeves, and behind him came Mr. Muller. He had come down to see the house, he said. The children all scrambled out so that he could see it better, and he walked around it smiling.

"That's a good little house," he said, patting

Freddie on the shoulder. "Freddie, when he grows up, shall be an architect like Papa."

"What about me, Papa? Will I be an architect too?" asked Tib.

"*Nein*, you will be a little housewife," said her father.

Betsy and Tacy thought that was strange, for Tib had done as much as Freddie toward building the house. But it didn't matter much, for in their hearts they were sure that Tib was going to be a dancer.

"And now," said Mr. Muller, "we must take this nice house down."

Nobody answered, and Mr. Muller looked around the circle. Betsy's face was very red, Tacy was hanging her head and Tib's round blue eyes were fixed on her father pleadingly. Freddie walked over to a corner of the basement. He pretended to be hunting for something.

Mr. Muller rubbed his mustache.

"Do you remember," he asked after a moment, "the story of the three little pigs?"

"Oh, yes," cried Betsy and Tacy and Tib.

"They built three little houses," said Tib's father, "and the Wolf knocked them down."

"That's right," said Betsy and Tacy and Tib all together.

"Very good," said Mr. Muller. "Well, you, Betsy and Tacy and Tib, are three little pigs. Only you have built just one house between you, just one little house, and this is it. And you, Freddie, are the Wolf, and you must knock it down."

"All right," cried Freddie, running back, forgetting to cry.

"I'm Whitey!" cried Tib, ruffling up her curls.

"I'm Blackie!" cried Betsy.

"I'm Reddie!" cried Tacy. (She couldn't be Brownie, because her hair was red.)

They rushed back inside the little house and

started pretending they were pigs.

Freddie came loping up to the doorway. He made his voice very sweet and soft.

"Little pig, little pig, let me come in."

Betsy and Tacy and Tib roared together.

"Not by the hair of my chinny-chin-chin."

Freddie roared back in the loudest voice he could find.

"Then I'll puff, and I'll huff, and I'll blow your house in."

He jumped around outside the little house, puffing and huffing, and Betsy and Tacy and Tib clung to each other and screamed.

"Watch out!" cried Mr. Muller. "Don't get hurt, anyone!"

Freddie puffed, and he huffed, and he huffed, and he puffed. At last he jumped straight into the little house and down it fell in chunks of wood around Betsy and Tacy and Tib. And he chased them through the basement, and he chased them up the stairs, and he chased them out to the knoll on the back lawn which was one of their favorite places to play. There they all fell down laughing underneath the oak tree.

But after they got rested they went on with the game. They pretended to do all the things the three little pigs in the story had done. They hunted for

turnips, and they hunted for apples, and they went
to the Fair.

It was a lovely game, and it lasted all afternoon.
It lasted until Julia and Katie came hunting for
Betsy and Tacy.

5
Everything Pudding

 HEN SCHOOL began Betsy and Tacy stopped every morning to call for Tib. At noon they all walked home together. And after dinner, when they went back to school, Betsy and Tacy called for Tib again. And after school at night they walked home together. But then they did not separate and go to their own homes; they usually went to one house to play.

Sometimes it was Tib's house, and sometimes it was Tacy's, and sometimes it was Betsy's. The place they went depended upon several things . . . upon the weather, upon whether they were playing outside or in, upon what the game required and upon what their mothers were doing. If a mother was cleaning house or having company, another mother's house was a better place to play. There wasn't any special invitation given. Not usually, that is.

But one day Betsy's mother said:

"Betsy, will you ask Mrs. Kelly and Mrs. Muller whether Tacy and Tib may come to play with you tomorrow after school? I am going to a party and I wish that Tacy and Tib could come and help you keep house."

"Will Julia be here?" asked Betsy.

"No," said her mother. "Julia will be taking her music lesson, and she is going to stay late to practise for the recital. Aunt Eva is going to look after Margaret for me, and Julia, Margaret and I will all come home with Papa."

"What time?" asked Betsy.

"About half-past five," said Mrs. Ray.

Betsy rushed out of the house to ask Mrs. Kelly if Tacy might come. Mrs. Kelly said she might. Then Betsy rushed to ask Mrs. Muller if Tib might come.

Mrs. Muller said she might. Betsy and Tacy and Tib thought it would be glorious to keep house all alone. They could hardly wait for the next day to come.

Next day after school Betsy came home alone, for Tacy and Tib . . . feeling something very special about the occasion . . . went home to clean up. They arrived about ten minutes later, by way of the front door, ringing the bell as though they were company.

Mrs. Ray was waiting for them, smelling of violet perfume. She was wearing a new tan dress with a high collar and wide yoke of brown velvet and bands of brown velvet around the billowy skirt. Her big hat was trimmed with brown velvet roses. She looked pretty.

"Now children," she said, "you know that you are not to touch the fires."

Of course they knew that; they had known that since they were babies.

"The back parlor stove and the kitchen range have both been fixed for the afternoon," she said. "Don't open a door or lift a lid."

They promised that they wouldn't.

"I've made some cocoa for you," Mrs. Ray said. "You'll find the pan on the back of the range. Just heat it up when you get hungry. There's a plateful of cupcakes to go with it. You may have a little party."

And Mrs. Ray put on her coat and her fur boa. (That smelled of violets too.) She kissed Betsy and said good-by to Tacy and Tib and went smiling out the door.

When the door had closed behind her the house seemed very still. It was so still that they felt they wanted to tiptoe when they walked. Tacy tiptoed to the piano and touched it. And Tib tiptoed over to Lady Jane Grey, the cat, and picked her up. And Betsy tiptoed to the window to look out.

It was snowing, and that made keeping house together all the nicer. Fleecy curtains of snow shut them into their warm, neat, quiet nest.

"What shall we do?" asked Tib.

"I think," said Betsy, "that we had better have our party."

Tacy and Tib thought so too.

They went out to the kitchen and Tib pulled the pan with cocoa in it to the warmest part of the stove. The fire was making small sociable noises. The tall clock on the kitchen shelf was ticking cheerfully. The table was set with a blue and white cloth and three blue and white napkins.

When the cocoa was hot they filled their cups and sat down at the table. They sipped their cocoa and ate their cupcakes with beautiful manners.

"We're getting pretty old when we can be left

alone like this," Betsy said.

"And warm up our own cocoa," said Tacy.

"Of course," said Tib, "I could have made the cocoa myself if your mamma had wanted me to. I know how to cook. I like to cook."

"I don't know how to cook," said Betsy. "But I think it's time I learned." She looked around the kitchen. "Do you know what I'd like to cook first?" she asked.

"What?" asked Tacy and Tib.

"It's called Everything," said Betsy. "It's called Everything because it's got everything in it." Tacy and Tib looked puzzled and Betsy explained. "A little bit of everything there is, cooked up in one pan. I think it would be delicious."

"I think it would be queer," said Tib.

"It *sounds* queer," said Tacy. "What would it be like, I wonder?"

"Well," said Betsy, looking at the ceiling. "I've never tasted it, of course. Nobody's ever tasted it, because nobody ever cooked it. We're inventing it right now. But I imagine that it would taste like everything good mixed together. Ice cream and blueberry pie and chicken with dumplings and lemonade and coffee cake . . ."

"Coffee cake is baked," said Tib.

"This wouldn't be baked," said Betsy, "because

Mamma said we weren't to open the oven door. But we could mix it in a pan and heat it on top of the stove the way we did the cocoa."

Tacy's blue eyes were sparkling.

"Why don't we?" she asked.

"Let's!" said Betsy.

So they put on aprons. Each one tied one of Betsy's mother's aprons around her neck, and Betsy got out a frying pan, the biggest one she could find.

"Now we mustn't put in much of any one thing," she warned. "Or else there won't be room. For we're going to put in *some* of *every thing*, absolutely everything there is. What shall we put in first?" she asked. She had never cooked before, and she didn't know how to begin.

"Bacon grease would be good," answered Tib. "Lots of things begin with bacon grease."

"Bacon grease then," said Betsy.

Tib went to the ice box and got a spoonful of bacon grease. It melted in the pan. Betsy added some sugar and Tacy poured in milk. They stirred it together well. Then Tib brought an egg and boldly broke it. Betsy and Tacy stared with admiration as it sloshed into the pan. Tacy put in flour and Betsy got some raisins.

"They ought to be washed first," said Tib. So Betsy washed them carefully and dropped them in.

Beside the big can of flour stood the cans of coffee and tea.

"Coffee ought to be boiled in a pot," objected Tib as Betsy approached them.

"Everything goes in together," said Betsy firmly. "Everything."

So coffee and tea were dumped into the pan.

"Here's tapioca," cried Tacy from the cupboard.

"Fine! Put it in!" cried Betsy.

"And cornstarch."

"Put it in."

"And gelatine. Gelatine's good," said Tacy.

"This is going to be good too, you bet," said Betsy, stirring.

"It doesn't look good yet," said Tib. "I believe it needs some soda." So she put in some soda.

They took turns stirring, and all three of them rummaged. Betsy put in cinnamon, and while the spices were out Tacy added ginger and allspice and cloves.

"Nutmeg needs to be grated," said Tib, so she grated nutmeg and sprinkled it in.

Tacy put in salt, and Tib put in pepper, and Betsy put in red pepper.

"I didn't know red pepper ... kerchew! ... made you sneeze so much ... kerchew! kerchew! ..." said Betsy, sneezing.

"I didn't know molasses was so sticky," said Tacy, pouring.

"I'll put in some bay leaves," said Tib. "Matilda often uses bay leaves."

The bay leaves floated strangely on the surface of the sticky mass.

They found the cruets of vinegar and olive oil. Betsy poured in vinegar and Tacy poured in olive oil. Tib added mustard and they stirred again.

They put in oatmeal, and cornmeal, and farina.

Tib was enjoying herself now. She was up on a chair poking into the upper shelves.

"Here's cocoanut. That's good."

"Hand it down," said Tacy.

"And chocolate and cocoa."

"Chocolate and cocoa," said Betsy, "is just what this needs."

They added butter and lard and an onion.

"My mother says an onion improves anything," said Betsy as she tossed it in.

They put in syrup and saleratus and baking powder. They put in rice and macaroni and citron. At last Tib said:

"Now it's time for flavoring, because we've put in everything there is, and flavoring always comes at the end. What kind shall we use?"

"Why, every kind," said Betsy. "Every kind there is."

"But Betsy, nobody uses more than one kind of flavoring."

"Nobody ever made this recipe before," said Betsy.

"What's the name of it?" asked Tib.

"Oh, its name is . . . let's see . . ." said Betsy.

"Everything Pudding would be good," said Tacy.

"That's right," said Betsy. "Its name is Everything Pudding."

And somehow that sounded like the first line of a song, and she began to hum it. She added a second line, and Tacy added a third, and Betsy chimed in with a fourth, and so on. They hummed it together, while Tib poured in the flavorings . . . vanilla and lemon and almond and rose. And Tib began to hum while she stirred, and pretty soon they were all singing together. The song went like this:

> *"Oh, its name is Everything Pudding,*
> *Its name is Everything Stew,*
> *Its name is Everything Cake or Pie,*
> *'Most any old name will do.*
> *It's better than strawberry shortcake,*
> *It's better than apple pie,*
> *It's better than chicken or ice cream or*
> *dumplings,*
> *We'll eat it bye and bye."*

They liked that song. And while the mixture simmered on the stove, and Tib stirred, they sang it lustily:

"Oh, its name is Everything Pudding,
Its name is Everything Stew . . ."

And when they came to the part where they named the things it was better than, they put in all the things they liked best . . . peach cobbler and sauerkraut and gingerbread and potato salad . . . but they always left apple pie at the end of one line for the sake of the rhyme.

They sang so loud that Lady Jane Grey began to yowl. She wasn't a very musical cat. Then Tib who was sniffing at the mixture said, "I'm sure it's done." And Betsy said, "All right. We'll eat." She brought three plates, and Tib spooned out some of the Everything Pudding (if that was what it was). And they sat down to eat it.

Betsy took a generous mouthful.

"It's perfectly delicious," she said. But she made a queer face.

Tacy took a mouthful, and when she had swallowed it she said, "It's lovely. But we put in just a little too much of something. Don't you think so, Betsy?"

"Yes," said Betsy. "I do."

Tib didn't say a thing. But before they had half finished what was on their plates, she put down her spoon and said, "I'm not going to eat any more."

"I don't care for any more either," said Betsy. "Let's give it to Lady Jane Grey."

The cat had been mewing and brushing against their legs, and she purred loudly as they put the Everything Pudding down on the floor. But when she had smelled it delicately, she walked away.

"Oh, well," said Betsy. "We'll just throw it out."

And she went out through the woodshed and scraped the Everything Something or Other into the pail.

"Now," said Tib, "we must clean up." And she took charge of things, for she was good at house work.

First she washed all the dishes, and Betsy and Tacy wiped them. Then she washed the pan and scrubbed off the stove and table. She even swept the floor. The broom was taller than Tib but she knew how to use it. She swept into every nook and corner.

It was growing dark and the kitchen looked as clean, almost, as it had been when they began.

The front door opened and Mr. and Mrs. Ray and Julia and Margaret came in. Mrs. Ray was smiling and looked pretty; she smelled of violet perfume.

"Did you have a good time, darlings?" she asked.

"Yes ma'am, we did," said Betsy, Tacy and Tib.

"Did you warm up your cocoa?" asked Julia, putting down her music roll.

"Yes, we did, and we ate up the cupcakes," Betsy answered.

"You left a nice clean kitchen," Mrs. Ray said. She walked around sniffing. "There's an odd smell though," she said.

Betsy and Tacy and Tib looked at each other. They were glad when Mr. Ray said, "Hop into your coats, T and T. I'll take you both home."

In the middle of the night that night, Tib had a stomach ache. She got up and went down to the kitchen and took a little soda. Tib knew that soda was good for stomach aches.

And Tacy had a stomach ache, and Katie took

care of her. Katie was bossy sometimes, but she was nice to have around when you felt sick.

And Betsy had a stomach ache, a bad one, and Julia was good to her too. But after Julia had given her peppermint and tucked her in, she said:

"Did you and Tacy and Tib have anything to eat besides those cupcakes and that cocoa?"

"Let's see!" said Betsy. "Did we or didn't we?"

After a moment she said, "Julia! Do you know what it would make if you took everything there is in the cupboard and cooked it up together?"

"Goodness!" said Julia. "You must be sick to think of such a thing!"

6

The Mirror Palace

NE DAY that winter, when Tib's mother
was going shopping, Betsy and Tacy and
Tib kept house alone at Tib's house. That
is, they were almost alone. Matilda was there but
she was taking care of Hobbie; and Freddie was
there, but he was out coasting on the knoll. Mrs.
Muller said that they could have the run of the

house. For Mrs. Ray had told her what good children they were when they kept house alone at Betsy's house.

"She said that you left the most spic and span kitchen!" Mrs. Muller said. "Well, good-by, my dears. Matilda has some nice fresh apple cake for you."

And Mrs. Muller went away downtown.

It was fun to have Tib's house all to themselves. Betsy and Tacy knew it well by now, but it still charmed them . . . the colored glass in the front door, the tower room with its blue velvet draperies, the back parlor with its broad window seat where they loved to sit and look at pictures of beautiful ladies in *Munsey's Magazine*.

The day they were left alone they found the most beautiful lady of all but she wasn't in a magazine.

Tib had taken them up to her mother's room to show them the new curtains. They were made of white lace over pale pink silk, threaded with pink satin ribbon and tied back with pink satin bows. The large room stretched across the front of the house, with an alcove beside it where Hobbie's bed was placed. Betsy and Tacy were roving about, admiring the curtains and the bureau with its bottles of perfume and the silver-backed mirrors and brushes, when Betsy picked up a framed photograph.

"Tib!" she cried. "Come here! Tell me who this is."

Her tone was so excited that Tacy came running

to look at the picture. Tib glanced at it and said:

"Why, that's Aunt Dolly."

"Your *aunt*?" asked Betsy. "Really? Did you ever actually *see* her?"

"Of course," said Tib. "I saw her every day when we lived in Milwaukee."

"Is she as beautiful as this?" asked Betsy.

Tib examined the photograph earnestly.

"Well, that looks just like her," she answered.

Betsy gazed, and Tacy gazed too. This was certainly a most beautiful lady. She was leaning against a marble pillar on which her elbow rested while her hand supported daintily her small exquisite head. A long train curled about her feet, making her slender rounded figure look as though it had been carved. She had masses of soft blonde hair and a doll-like face.

"She looks like Tib," said Tacy.

"Yes, she does," said Betsy.

"I'm supposed to look like her," said Tib. "But I don't expect I'll ever be that pretty."

Betsy and Tacy turned to look at her.

"You're quite pretty now, Tib," Betsy said.

"Especially when you're dressed up," said Tacy.

"I'm too tanned," said Tib.

She picked up her mother's mirror and inspected her small tanned face while Betsy and Tacy gazed at the photograph, heaving great sighs of admiration.

But they couldn't look at the photograph forever, so at last they put it down. Tib was still gazing into the mirror.

"I'm not looking at myself any more," she explained. "I'm looking at the ceiling. It looks different in the mirror. See?"

She handed the mirror to Betsy and Tacy and they peered in. Sure enough, the ceiling did look different. It didn't look like a ceiling. It looked like the floor of a new mysterious room.

"It's a Mirror Room," Betsy said.

The Mirror Room was carpeted with tiny pink flowers, for the ceiling wall paper was covered with tiny pink flowers. They matched the big pink flowers which twined around silver poles on the walls of the room. At the top of the wall, next to the ceiling, was a border with silver leaves and large and small pink flowers all together. If you tilted the mirror just a little, you could see that border.

Holding the mirror between them, and looking down into its depths, Betsy and Tacy started to walk. They walked around the room and into the alcove, bumping a bit, but that didn't matter; Hobbie wasn't in his bed; he was down in the kitchen watching Matilda iron.

"It's fun walking through this Mirror Room. You try it," said Betsy, offering the mirror to Tib.

"I'll go get mirrors for us all," said Tib. And she did. She brought her father's shaving mirror for Tacy and Matilda's mirror for herself. Matilda's mirror was a big square mirror in a dark brown frame. It was heavy. But Tib didn't mind.

They walked out into the hall, looking in their mirrors as they went.

"We'll explore this whole Mirror Palace," Betsy said. "That's what it is . . . a Mirror Palace."

"Who lives in it?" asked Tacy.

"Aunt Dolly," said Betsy. "She's the Queen."

Tib was so surprised that she almost dropped Matilda's mirror. She stared at Betsy with her round blue eyes.

"Why, Betsy!" she cried. "My Aunt Dolly lives in a flat in Milwaukee."

"She used to, maybe," Betsy said.

"But I'd know if she lived in this house," said Tib.

"The Mirror Palace has no connection with this house," said Betsy.

"Oh," said Tib. She still looked surprised, but she was beginning to get used to Betsy. She had played with her for two whole years. So when Tacy said, "Come on! Let's explore the Mirror Palace," Tib said, "All right." They formed a line and descended the stairs, each holding fast to her mirror with one hand and grasping the rail with the other.

In the downstairs hall the floor of the Palace was leathery brown. That was because the ceiling wall paper was leathery brown. In the front and back parlors, the floor became delicately blue, with darker blue scrolls visible when you tilted the mirror just a little. The dining room was the nicest of all. There the floor was thrillingly red and gold.

"This is the Throne Room," Betsy said, and they walked around the Throne Room. "Now," she continued, "we'll inspect the Royal Kitchens."

They started toward the kitchen but Tib checked them.

"We'd better not go out there," she said. "Matilda's ironing. Maybe she wouldn't like this walking around with mirrors. Especially when one of them's hers."

"Maybe not," Betsy and Tacy agreed.

"Anyway," said Tacy, looking around the dining room with its rich red and gold walls, the sideboard laden with silver and the long table spread with a heavy woven cloth and a silver dish filled with oranges, "Anyway I think it would be fun to play right here in the Throne Room."

"Oh yes!" cried Betsy. "We'll make a throne for Aunt Dolly."

"But where *is* Aunt Dolly?" asked Tib.

"When you look in the mirror," said Betsy, "that makes Aunt Dolly."

Betsy pulled out Tib's father's armchair which sat at the head of the table, and Tib ran to get her mother's paisley shawl. It was old; she was allowed to play with it. They draped it over the chair and pushed the chair up against the window. The window's red draperies made a majestic background.

Tacy was inspecting the sideboard.

"Some of this silver would come in handy around a throne," she said. "But maybe we shouldn't touch it."

"We'll put it all back," Betsy said.

"You decorate while I get something," said Tib. She ran away and came back wearing her mother's feather boa.

At the right of the throne Betsy and Tacy had put the silver coffee urn; at the left, the silver teapot.

"She can use this big ladle for a sceptre," said Betsy. "But what will we do for a crown?"

"The sugar bowl's a good shape," said Tacy. "But it's full of sugar lumps."

"The spoon holder," said Betsy, "is just the thing."

So they dumped out the tea spoons and clamped the spoon holder upside down upon Tib's head. Her little yellow curls sprang out beneath the silver bowl. With the fluffy feather boa she looked supremely queenlike.

"Now look into your mirror and you'll turn into Queen Dolly," Betsy cried.

Tib looked into the mirror and Betsy took the silver fruit dish and went down upon one knee.

"Will your Majesty deign to eat an orange?" she asked.

Tacy began to giggle as she seized the sugar bowl and bowed.

"Some sugar, I prithee, Queen," she said.

Queen Dolly crooked her little finger and accepted an orange and a sugar lump.

Just then Freddie burst in through the swinging door. He had left his sled outside, of course, and his rubbers beside the kitchen door, and his coat and cap and muffler in the kitchen closet, but his pink cheeks brought in the out-of-doors.

"Whatcha playing?" he asked.

"We're playing Mirror Palace," Betsy answered. "Tib's playing she's Aunt Dolly."

"And Aunt Dolly's the Queen," Tacy explained.

Freddie looked puzzled. He knew how to play that someone was another person, but he hadn't ever played that someone was *two* other persons. He thought he had better change the subject.

"We're not supposed to play in the dining room," he said.

"Why, Freddie!" Betsy cried. "We're not playing in the dining room. This is the Throne Room." And she explained about the Mirror Palace. Freddie looked down into the mirror Tib was holding, and he could see for himself what a shining mysterious room the mirror held.

"But Tib ought to be upside down," he remarked.

"What?" exclaimed Betsy and Tacy.

"Her feet ought to be on the Mirror Palace floor."

Betsy and Tacy looked dismayed. It was perfectly true. If the ceiling of the dining room, reflected in the mirror, was the floor of the Mirror Palace, then Tib's reflected feet ought to be where her head was.

"You ought to be standing on your head," said Betsy.

"That's easy," said Tib.

For Tib was a dancer. It wasn't a bit of trouble for Tib to stand on her head. She took off her spoonholder crown and put Matilda's mirror carefully on the seat of the throne. She jumped to the arms of the chair and went upside down, her head upon the mirror, her legs stretching straight and true into the air.

Betsy and Tacy and Freddie, looking down into the mirror, had a fleeting dazzling vision . . . Queen Dolly with her dainty feet pointing toward the floor. But the vision was fleeting, indeed!

The kitchen door swung open and Matilda, her arms full of freshly ironed linen, entered the dining room.

"Gott im Himmel!" cried Matilda, and table-cloths and napkins fell in a snowy shower.

Tib came rightside up in a hurry. She came in such a hurry that she tumbled to the floor. The coffee urn crashed, and so did the teapot . . . they were silver, so they didn't break. Oranges rolled in all directions.

But Matilda was looking at the mirror.

"Whose mirror is that?" she demanded.

"It's yours, Matilda," said Tib. "I borrowed it for this game we were playing."

"We were going to put everything back, Matilda," Betsy said.

Tacy was already picking up the linen and Freddie was pursuing oranges.

Matilda examined the mirror.

"It isn't broken. No thanks to you," she said.

"We're glad it isn't broken, Matilda," Betsy said. And she and Tacy folded the linen so neatly, you would not have known it had fallen, hardly. Freddie had found all the oranges, so now he was picking up silver. Tib put the feather boa and the paisley shawl away.

Matilda stalked back to the kitchen.

Working silently and swiftly, Betsy and Tacy and Tib and Freddie put the dining room to rights. It looked so tidy when they had finished that no one would dream it had ever been mussed up. Then they went to the window seat and sat down softly.

"I wonder if we'll get the apple cake," asked Freddie in a whisper.

"Probably not," said Tib.

"Never mind," said Betsy. "I'll tell you a story about Aunt Dolly and how she happens to live in a mirror."

So she told them the story while twilight spread purple gauze over the drifts outside.

But before she had finished Matilda brought them the apple cake. They could hardly believe their eyes when she stalked in with the tray.

"Thank you, Matilda," said Tib. "I'm glad your mirror wasn't broken."

"So'm I," Tacy murmured.

"The dining room looks all right now," Betsy added. "Doesn't it, Matilda?"

Matilda looked at the tidy dining room. She swept it with a stony glance.

"I hear," she said meaningly, "that Mrs. Ray's kitchen looked nice *too* after you kept house for *her* one day."

And she stalked back into the kitchen.

7

Red Hair, Yellow Hair, and Brown

THAT SPRING Tacy had diphtheria.

Betsy and Tacy and Tib had always thought that spring was the nicest part of the year; but it wasn't much fun that year; it wasn't much fun without Tacy.

The snow melted up on the Big Hill and came rushing down the slopes in foaming torrents. And Betsy and Tib made boats and sent them bobbing down the stream to the Atlantic and the Pacific. They did it every year; it was one of their favorite things to do; but it wasn't much fun without Tacy.

May Day came, and of course they made baskets. They made them out of tissue paper in all the colors of the rainbow; beautiful baskets with fringed paper trimming and braided paper handles. And they filled the baskets with spring flowers from the chilly snow-patched hills, and hung them on people's door knobs; and rang the bells and ran away. But it wasn't much fun without Tacy.

The trees on the hill turned slowly green and the wild plum was dazzlingly white and fragrant, and gardens were planted, and birds came back, and the last day of school arrived. Betsy and Tib emptied their desks. . . . Betsy emptied Tacy's desk too . . . and she brought home Tacy's books as well as her own. She and Tib marched home with their arms full of books singing loudly:

> "No more Latin,
> No more French,
> No more sitting on a
> Hardwood bench. . . ."

But it wasn't much fun without Tacy. At least not so much fun as it would have been *with* Tacy. Betsy and Tib would forget and have fun, and then they would remember that Tacy had diphtheria.

Fortunately, by that time she was almost well. People had stopped looking sober when you mentioned Tacy's name. Tacy's father and her big brother George and her grown-up sister Mary called out jokes when they saw Betsy and Tib, and the other brothers and sisters laughed and played on the lawn. They couldn't leave the yard for they were quarantined with Tacy. "Quarantined" meant that they had to stay at home in order not to give anybody diphtheria. While Tacy was so sick they had to play quiet games, but now they could make all the noise they liked.

Tacy got so well that she could come to the window. She would hold up that doll George had given her at the Street Fair and make it wave its hands. Betsy and Tib sent her gifts on the end of a fish pole. They would tie the gift on the end of a pole and poke the pole over into Tacy's yard and Katie would untie it and take it to Tacy. They sent notes and stories and pieces of cake and bouquets of flowers and a turtle.

At last Tacy got well, as well as anybody, but she was still in quarantine. She sat on the porch and she walked around the yard, and Betsy and Tib could shout at her but they couldn't play with her. They stood on the hitching block and shouted, and she came as near them as she was allowed to come. They could see how tall she had grown and how pale. Her freckles were almost gone, and the paleness made her eyes look big and blue.

"Tacy's pretty," Betsy said to Tib. "She's almost as pretty as you are."

"Yes, she is," Tib agreed.

One day over at Tacy's house there was a great deal of sweeping and scrubbing. Piles of trash were burned in the back yard and a man came to fumigate. That meant that he filled the house with a cleansing smoke. The next day the quarantine ended.

The minute it was ended Betsy and Tib ran over to see Tacy. The three of them ran around the yard and jumped over Mrs. Kelly's peony bed and ran down to the pump and pumped water and splashed and yelled with joy. Mrs. Kelly came out on the porch and watched them, and she was smiling but she looked as though she wanted to cry. That trembling look she had on her face made Betsy feel funny. It gave her an idea.

She didn't mention her idea for a while, there were so many things to do. Tacy could leave her own yard now; she didn't need to stay there any more; so Betsy took hold of one of her hands and Tib took hold of the other and they went to all their favorite places. They went to the bench at the top of Hill Street, and they went to Betsy's backyard maple, and they went to the ridge where wild roses were in bloom.

They were sitting down on the ridge resting and smelling the roses when Betsy mentioned her idea.

"I've been thinking," she said. "I've been thinking a lot this morning. I've got an idea."

"What is it?" asked Tacy and Tib.

"I've been thinking," said Betsy, "that Tacy was pretty sick. And if she had died we wouldn't have had a thing to remember her by."

"I'd've remembered her," said Tib.

"And anyhow I didn't die," said Tacy. "But I was certainly pretty sick. I was so sick the doctor came every day. I was so sick it's all mixed up, like a dream. What's your idea, Betsy? I'll bet it's a good one."

"It's this," said Betsy. "We three ought to have something to remember each other by. You got sick, Tacy, and I might get sick too, any day. I might get sick and die."

"I hope you won't," said Tib, looking worried.

"You might yourself," answered Betsy. "You might get sick just the same as Tacy did, and you might die. We certainly ought to have something to remember each other by."

"I think I'd remember you, Betsy," said Tib. "I'm sure I would. Wouldn't you remember me?"

"Well," said Betsy, "it wouldn't hurt to have

some special thing to help me. Like my Grandma's got something to remember my Grandpa by."

"What's she got?" asked Tacy.

"It's a piece of his hair," said Betsy. "It was cut off his head, and she wears it in a locket."

Tacy and Tib looked impressed.

"We'll get us some lockets," said Betsy. "And we'll put in our lockets a piece of all our hairs. We could sort of braid them together. They'd look nice because Tacy's is red, and yours, Tib, is yellow, and mine is brown."

"They'd certainly look nice," said Tacy.

"But we haven't got any lockets," said Tib.

"No," said Betsy. "But we could cut off the hair. We could get that much done right away. I'll run down and ask my mamma for some scissors."

"And we'll try to think what we can use for lockets," Tacy said.

Betsy jumped up and ran down the hill to her house. Her mother was in the kitchen making a cake, and she was pretty busy. She was beating eggs as fast as she could.

"How's Tacy?" she called out over the noise of the egg beater. "Is she glad to be out?"

"Yes," said Betsy. "And we need some scissors for something we're doing. May I take the scissors, please?"

"Yes," said her mother. "You may take the blunt pair I let you cut paper dolls with. Hold the points down, and don't run."

And she finished beating her eggs and began sifting flour. Betsy took the scissors and went out the kitchen door.

Tacy and Tib called out as she came near.

"We've been thinking," Tacy said, "what we could use for lockets. We won't be able to afford lockets for a while. But do you know what we could use?"

"Pill boxes," said Tib without waiting for Betsy to answer. "They're just the right shape."

"While I was sick," said Tacy, "our house was full of pill boxes, but my mother burned them all up yesterday."

"We have a few pill boxes at our house," Betsy said. "Maybe some of them are empty."

"And Mrs. Benson would have some pill boxes, I imagine," Tacy said. "Tib and I will go and ask her while you ask your mother."

Tacy and Tib ran down the street to Mrs. Benson's and Betsy ran into the house to her mother again. Her mother had finished sifting flour now. She was beating the cake hard.

"Mamma," said Betsy. "Have you any old empty pill boxes Tacy and Tib and I could have?"

"What do you want pill boxes for?" her mother

asked, sounding surprised.

"To make lockets of," said Betsy. "We're going to punch holes and run strings through and hang them around our necks."

"Oh," said Mrs. Ray. "Well, I think I've got a pill box somewhere. Just wait a minute, and I'll see." And she scraped the cake into the pan and popped the pan into the oven and went into the bedroom. Before Betsy had finished cleaning out the bowl and Margaret had finished licking the spoon, she was back with one pill box.

"That's all I could find," she said. "There's some string on the clock shelf."

Betsy took the pill box and the ball of string and ran back to the ridge. Tacy and Tib had just come back from Mrs. Benson's, and they had two pill boxes, beautiful ones.

"We told her we were going to make lockets," Tacy said. "She thought it was a fine idea."

So they took the scissors and punched holes in the pill boxes, and they ran string through them and tied them around each other's necks. They made lovely lockets.

"Now," said Betsy, "it's time to cut off the hair." And she picked up the scissors.

"Who'll cut it?" asked Tacy. "I think we should take turns, because cutting hair will be fun."

"That's right," said Betsy. "Well, I'll cut yours, and you can cut Tib's, and Tib can cut mine."

She walked around Tacy looking at her hair and trying to decide where to begin. Tacy's hair, as usual, was dressed in ringlets. There were ten long red ringlets, as neat as sausages.

"I'll begin on this one," said Betsy, and she lifted up a ringlet right next to Tacy's face. She cut it off close to the head.

The shimmering long red ringlet looked beautiful on the grass.

"I think I'll cut off another one," Betsy said. And she did.

"It makes her look funny," Tib said, staring at Tacy.

"That's right," said Betsy. "I'd better cut off exactly half. Then it will look neater."

So she cut off three more ringlets, one after another. Exactly half were gone. And one side of Tacy's head had five short stubs of curls while the other side had five long ringlets.

"Well, that's done," said Betsy, and she handed the scissors to Tacy.

Tacy walked around Tib looking at her hair. The short yellow curls would not be so easy to cut.

"They're not so regular," said Tacy. "But I'll try to cut off exactly half."

She began at Tib's left ear and cut off all the curls on the left side of her head. Shining yellow rings showered the ground.

Then Tib took the scissors and walked around Betsy.

"Betsy's easy," she said. "She's got two braids, and I'll cut off one."

She unbraided one braid and cut off the hair which had made it. Unbraided, Betsy's hair looked crinkly; it was almost as curly as Tacy's and Tib's.

They put all the hair they had cut in a row on the grass. Red ringlets, short yellow curls, crinkly brown hair. They divided it into three equal piles, and each one took a pile. But the piles were much too big to stuff into a pill box. The pill boxes wouldn't hold a fraction of what they had cut. They filled them as full as they could, and they spread the rest of the hair on the wild rose bushes.

"The birds can use that hair in their nests," Tacy said. "I once saw a bird carrying hair."

They played around the rose bushes a while but the more they looked at each other, the funnier each one thought the other two looked. They began to be a little worried about going home.

"Let's go all together," said Betsy. "Three can explain things better than one."

So they took hold of hands, very tightly, and went down the hill.

They went to Betsy's house first. And when Betsy's mother saw them she shrieked. Grown-ups don't often shriek, but that was what Betsy's mother did.

"Betsy!" she cried. "Tacy! Tib! Whatever have you done to yourselves!"

"We've cut off our hair," said Betsy.

"But why? What for?" cried Betsy's mother.

"To remember each other by," said Betsy.

"That's nonsense!" cried Betsy's mother. And she put down her knife . . . she had been frosting the cake . . . but she didn't offer a speck of the frosting to anybody. She took off her apron and lifted up

Margaret, who was staring at Betsy with eyes like saucers. "You come along with me," she said, and Mrs. Ray and Margaret and Betsy and Tacy and Tib went across the street to Mrs. Kelly's.

Mrs. Kelly was sweeping the walk. She saw them coming, and after she had looked at them hard she threw her apron over her head. When she took down the apron she was crying. She ran her hand over Tacy's head and said, "Oh those beautiful long red ringlets! Those beautiful long red ringlets!" She felt bad.

"I'm so sorry, Mrs. Kelly," Mrs. Ray said. "I'm sure it was Betsy's idea."

"We did it to remember each other by," said Tacy.

But nobody seemed to pay any attention.

Julia and Katie had been playing hop scotch. They ran to see what was the matter.

"Well, for goodness' sake!" they cried. "For goodness' sake!"

Paul had been racing two carts down the terrace. He ran to see what was the matter too.

Mrs. Kelly wiped her eyes and took off her apron.

"I'll go along with you to Mrs. Muller's," she said to Mrs. Ray.

And Mrs. Ray and Mrs. Kelly and Julia and Katie and Paul and Margaret and Betsy and Tacy and Tib went down the street and through the vacant lot to Mrs. Muller's.

"I'm glad you're all coming along," said Tib.

And it was a good thing that there were plenty of people on hand to explain to Mrs. Muller. For Mrs. Muller didn't like it at all that half of Tib's hair was cut off. Mrs. Muller was proud of Tib. She was proud of how pretty and dainty she was, and of

how she could dance. She was proud of her yellow curls.

At sight of those shorn yellow curls Mrs. Muller turned white. She stood up . . . she had been embroidering a dress for Tib under the oak tree on the knoll.

"Tib," she said. "Go to your room. You are going to be punished."

"Mrs. Muller," said Mrs. Ray, "I am so afraid this is one of Betsy's ideas. Let's talk it all over."

"Let's find out what they did it for," Mrs. Kelly said.

"All right," said Mrs. Muller.

Betsy swallowed. She swallowed hard.

"I thought," she said, "that we ought to have some of each other's hair to remember each other by."

"It's because I was so sick," said Tacy.

"And I might get sick too," said Tib, "and so might Betsy."

"So we cut off a little of each other's hair to put in our lockets," explained Betsy.

And they showed their mothers their pill boxes full of brown and red and yellow hair.

Mrs. Ray looked at the pill boxes and she began to laugh. She had been very angry, but she could get over being angry fast. Mr. Ray said it was on account of her hair, which was red like Tacy's. Mrs. Kelly began to laugh too, although she was wiping her eyes again. And at last Mrs. Muller began to laugh. She called Freddie.

"Freddie," she said, "will you ask Matilda to bring me the scissors, please?"

And Matilda brought the scissors, and Mrs. Muller cut off what was left of Tacy's long red ringlets and of Tib's short yellow curls and she cut off Betsy's one remaining braid.

"At least," she said as she clipped, "it is summer time. And short hair will be cool. But just the same," she said to Tib, "you are going to be punished."

"And so is Betsy," said Mrs. Ray, "very severely too."

"And so is Tacy," Mrs. Kelly added.

But Mrs. Kelly hated to punish Tacy because she had had the diphtheria. She took Tacy's long red ringlets and put them in a candy box and kept them in a bureau drawer.

8

Being Good

T WAS strange that Betsy and Tacy and Tib ever did things which grown-ups thought were naughty, for they tried so hard to be good. They were very religious. Betsy was a Baptist, and Tacy was a Catholic, and Tib was an Episcopalian.

They loved to sit on Tacy's back fence and talk about God.

Tacy's back fence was a very good place for such talk. There wasn't a soul around to listen except the cow, and sometimes the horse, munching and stamping behind them. And above the crowding treetops there was a fine view of sky, the place where God lived.

Betsy and Tacy and Tib were talking about Him one morning. They were looking up at the great fleecy clouds sailing across the sky.

"It will be fun living up there after we die," Betsy said. "We'll all be so beautiful . . . we'll look like Aunt Dolly."

"Tib looks like her already," Tacy said.

"Not since I got my hair cut," said Tib. "I'm not very pretty since I got my hair cut."

There was a pause.

"Well, you'll have long hair in Heaven," Betsy said. "All of us will. We'll all be beautiful. And we'll sail around with palm leaves in our hands. They have good things to eat in Heaven, I imagine. They have ice cream and cake for breakfast even."

"I'd like that," said Tib.

"We have to be good though," Tacy said, "or else we won't go there."

"We're pretty good already," Betsy said. "We're lots better than Julia and Katie. Getting up a Club and not inviting us!"

"The stuck-up things!" Tacy said.

Betsy and Tacy and Tib all covered their mouths with their hands and stuck out their tongues three times. They had made an agreement to do this, in public or in private, whenever Julia's and Katie's Club was mentioned. Julia's and Katie's Club was called the B.H.M. Club. No one under ten years of age had been invited to join. The meetings were held on the Big Hill every Tuesday afternoon. And this was Tuesday morning.

"I know what let's do!" cried Betsy. "Let's get up a Club ourselves."

"Let's get up a Club about being good," suggested Tacy.

"That doesn't sound like fun," said Tib.

"Well, we can't think about fun all the time if we want to go to Heaven," said Betsy.

"That's right," said Tacy. "The saints didn't have much fun; I'll tell you that. They used to wear hair shirts."

"Did they?" asked Betsy. "What for?"

"To punish themselves. To make themselves gooder. And if they did anything bad they put pebbles in their shoes."

"What else did they do?" Betsy asked.

Tacy looked at her suspiciously.

"You're not thinking about doing things like that

in our Club, are you, Betsy?" she asked.

"Not exactly," said Betsy. She sat thinking, her bare toes curled around a wooden bar of the fence.

"My mamma wouldn't let me wear any different kind of shirt," said Tib. She sounded as though she didn't like the Club.

"Don't worry," said Betsy. "We wouldn't know where to buy hair shirts, even. Besides, we haven't got any money. What would be a good name for our Club, do you suppose?"

They all thought hard.

Betsy suggested The Christian Kindness Club. And they liked that name because it made such nice initials. Clubs were called by their initials, for their names were kept secret. T.C.K.C. sounded fine.

"What shall we do in our Club?" asked Tib. She still sounded as though she didn't like it. But Tib always did what Betsy and Tacy wanted to do. She was very pleasant to play with. "Will we have refreshments?" she asked, cheering up.

"No," said Betsy. "This is a pretty serious Club, this T.C.K.C."

"It's about being good," said Tacy.

"And we'll never get to be good if we don't punish ourselves for being bad. A child could see that," said Betsy. "So in our Club we'll punish ourselves for being bad."

"But we haven't been bad yet," said Tib. "I wasn't even intending to be bad."

"We were born bad," said Tacy. "Everyone is. Go on, Betsy."

"The pebbles gave me the idea," said Betsy. "We'll take our marble bags and empty out the marbles and pin the bags inside our dresses."

Tib looked uncomfortable. "Doesn't that remind you of those pill boxes?" she asked. "There isn't any cutting off hair in this Club, is there, Betsy?"

"Of course not," said Betsy. "This is a Being Good Club. We're going to put stones in those bags around our necks."

"Oh," said Tib.

"Every time we do anything bad," continued Betsy, "we'll put a stone in. If we're very bad, we'll have to put in two stones, or three. By tonight those bags will be bulging full, I imagine . . ."

"I wouldn't wonder," said Tacy, her eyes sparkling.

"I don't see why," said Tib. "I thought we were going to be *good*."

Just then the whistles blew for twelve o'clock. And Betsy and Tacy and Tib flew in three directions.

"We'll meet on my hitching block right after dinner. Bring your bags," cried Betsy, as she flew.

Betsy hurried through her dinner. Julia was hurrying too, for the B.H.M. Club, so she said, met that afternoon. When Julia said that, Betsy lifted her napkin and poked out her tongue three times.

"Did you choke on something, Betsy?" her father asked.

"No sir," said Betsy. "Mamma, it's Julia's turn to wipe the dishes."

"Yes," said her mother, "and you may look after Margaret for me until it's time for her nap."

While Julia was wiping the dishes, Betsy hunted up her marbles bag. She emptied the marbles into a box, and pinned the bag inside her red plaid dress. It made a bump on her chest. Taking Margaret's chubby hand, she ran out to the hitching block as fast as Margaret's chubby legs would go.

Tacy was already there, and Tib was in sight, wheeling Hobbie's gocart up the hill.

There was a bump on Tib's chest beneath her yellow dimity dress; and there was a bump on Tacy's chest too beneath her striped blue and brown gingham. While they were admiring one another's bumps Julia and Katie started up the hill, carrying lunch baskets, and a stick and a square flat package which they always took to their Club.

Betsy made a face at them. It was a regular monkey

face, the kind her mother had said she should not make for fear her face would freeze that way.

"Oh dear!" she said. "Now I've been bad. I must put a stone in my bag."

And she found a pebble and put it into her bag.

"I think I'd better put a stone in my bag too," said Tacy. "Because when Katie told me she was going to her Club I called her stuck up."

So Tacy put a pebble in *her* bag.

Tib ran to the foot of the hill and called loudly after Julia and Katie.

"You're stuck up! You're stuck up!"

And *she* put a pebble in *her* bag.

Margaret and Hobbie began shouting too. "'tuck up! 'tuck up!" But they didn't understand about the pebbles.

Betsy's mother came to the door of the little yellow cottage.

"Betsy! Betsy! What are you playing?"

"This is our Club, Mamma. We've got a Club too. This is our T.C.K.C. Club."

"What do you do in your Club?" asked Mrs. Ray.

"Oh," said Betsy. "We see how good we can be."

"Well, there's certainly no harm in that," said her mother. She went back into the house.

But the Club didn't work out exactly as they had expected. The little bags didn't make them want to be good; it was too much fun putting in the stones.

Tib climbed up on the rain barrel and drabbled the skirts of her yellow dimity dress . . . two stones.

Tacy climbed the backyard maple and swung by her knees from a branch; her mother had said this was dangerous . . . one stone.

Betsy ran into the kitchen and got cookies without asking . . . one stone.

Margaret ran happily screaming in a circle. Hobbie bounced up and down in the gocart and yelled.

"'tone! 'tone!" cried Margaret and Hobbie. For even Margaret and Hobbie knew now that stones were part of the game. But Betsy, Tacy and Tib didn't give them any stones. They didn't pay any attention to them.

Betsy's mother came to the door again.

"A little less noise would be *very* good," she said.

"Yes, ma'am," said Betsy.

But it was such fun putting stones in their bags. They grew naughtier and naughtier.

Tacy picked a bouquet of her mother's zinnias. Betsy filled the pockets of her red plaid dress with mud. Tib jumped into the seat of the baker's wagon, which was standing in front of Mrs. Benson's house while the baker's boy offered his tray of jelly rolls and doughnuts at Mrs. Benson's back door. She took up the reins and took up the whip and pretended she was going to drive off. She scared the baker's boy almost to death.

Betsy's mother came to the door again and said that she thought they were possessed. Tacy's mother came to *her* door and told Tacy to be a good girl. And Tib's mother would have come to *her* door too, only Tib's house was so far away that her mother didn't know a thing about what was going on.

The bags on their chests grew bigger and bigger. At last they were almost full.

Tacy sat down on the hitching block, red-faced from laughing.

"Gol darn!" she said distinctly.

"*Tacy!*" cried Betsy. "That's *swearing*. That earns you three stones."

Tacy was proud to be the first to get three stones. The three stones filled her bag.

Betsy looked around for something she could do to earn three stones. She saw her mother's golf cape airing on the line, and she took it down and put it on and walked to the corner and back.

"That earns me three stones too," she said, taking it off quickly.

"I know how I can earn three stones," cried Tib. "Just watch me!"

She ran out into Betsy's father's garden and began to pick tomatoes.

"That's three stones all right," said Betsy, when Tib returned with the red tomatoes in her skirt.

Now all this time Margaret and Hobbie had been just as bad as they knew how. They had screamed and yelled and kicked and jumped, but no one had given them a single stone. Perhaps Margaret and Hobbie thought that they hadn't been bad enough. Or perhaps they just liked the looks of the ripe red tomatoes. At any rate Hobbie took a tomato and threw it at Margaret.

Margaret was delighted when the soft tomato broke in a big red splotch on her dress. She threw one at Hobbie. Hobbie threw one at Tacy and Margaret

threw one at Betsy and they both threw one at Tib.

"'tone! 'tone!" cried Hobbie, smearing tomato into his pale yellow hair.

"'tone! 'tone!" shrieked Margaret, rubbing the red juice into her chubby cheeks.

"Oh! Oh! Oh!" cried Betsy and Tacy and Tib.

Betsy's mother came out just then. And after that the Club wasn't much fun for a while. Betsy and Margaret were motioned into the house in a terrible silence, and the door closed behind them. Tacy was called home, and the door closed behind her too. And Tib took Hobbie home, but she cleaned him up first, the best she could, at Tacy's pump.

Down on the back fence behind Tacy's barn that night, Betsy, Tacy and Tib counted their stones. Tib had the most. But when they were counted she threw them away.

"I think," she said, "that we'd better use these bags for marbles again. We seem to get into trouble when we tie things around our necks."

"That's right. We do," said Tacy. And she threw away her stones too.

"Maybe we'd better change our Club a little," Tacy said, "have our meetings up on the Big Hill."

"Have refreshments," said Tib.

"Take lunch baskets up," said Tacy.

"And a stick and a package, maybe," said Tib.

"What do you think, Betsy?" Tacy asked. For Betsy had not yet thrown away her stones. She was looking up at the western sky where a pale green lake was surrounded by peach-colored mountains, distant and mysterious.

"All right," said Betsy, and she threw away her stones. "But of course we must keep on being good."

"Oh, of course!" said Tacy.

"That's what our Club is for," added Betsy.

"It's a Being Good Club," Tacy said.

"Well, it didn't make us good today," said Tib. "It made us bad."

Neither Betsy nor Tacy would have mentioned that. But they didn't mind Tib's mentioning it. They understood Tib.

In silence the three of them looked at the sunset and thought about God.

9
The Secret Lane

FROM THAT time on T.C.K.C. meetings were held on the Big Hill. Every Tuesday Julia and Katie went up on the Big Hill for a meeting of their B.H.M. Club. And every Tuesday Betsy and Tacy and Tib climbed the hill for T.C.K.C. meetings. Yet not once had Betsy and Tacy and Tib caught a glimpse of Julia and Katie. That shows how big the Big Hill was.

Betsy and Tacy and Tib did different things at their meetings. . . . They always took a picnic lunch, of course; but they didn't take a stick and a package, for they didn't know what Julia and Katie did at their Club with a stick and a package. They couldn't imagine. Sometimes Betsy and Tacy and Tib called on Mrs. Ekstrom and laughed about that day when they had pretended they were beggars. And sometimes they turned left at the top of the hill and walked to that lofty rim from which they had a view over the town and the river. But one day they turned right.

Here the Big Hill stretched away to the south. Flat and grassy and dotted with trees, the top of the Big Hill stretched to they didn't know where. Betsy and Tacy and Tib decided to walk in that direction. They walked and they walked and they walked.

They were carrying a picnic basket; and although they took turns carrying it, it grew heavy at last. The day was warm and they were almost ready to stop and eat their lunch beneath the shade of the trees when Tib made a discovery.

"Look!" she said. "These trees aren't just scattered every which way any more."

"They're going in two rows," said Tacy.

"It's a lane!" cried Betsy. She stopped still. They all

stopped, and they looked before and behind them.

Sure enough, it was a lane. The trees were no longer scattered oaks and elms and maples; they were all beech trees and they were planted in two rows. The rows ran as straight as though they had been laid down with a ruler. They ran like two lines of marching soldiers . . . where?

"Where do you suppose this lane leads to?" Tacy asked.

"There isn't any house up on the Big Hill, except the Ekstroms'," Tib said.

Betsy peered down the mysterious shadowy lane.

"Maybe Aunt Dolly lives up here," she said.

"Oh no," said Tib. "She lives in Milwaukee."

"She *used* to live in Milwaukee," said Tacy. "That doesn't mean she will live there forever."

"Well, she lives in Milwaukee now," said Tib. "Because my mamma had a letter from her. She's coming to visit us."

"What?" cried Betsy.

"You never told us!" cried Tacy.

"I was going to tell you," said Tib. "But this Aunt Dolly who's coming to visit us . . . she's just Aunt Dolly. She doesn't live in a mirror or up in the sky or here in this lane or anything. Does she, Betsy?" Tib looked puzzled.

"Wait and see," said Betsy. "When's she coming?"

"Next week," said Tib.

"Tib!" cried Betsy and Tacy.

They could hardly believe their good luck.

"We can see her!" cried Betsy.

"We'll come over and peek," said Tacy.

"Oh, I'll invite you in," said Tib. "You can come in and talk to her."

"I'd be scared to," said Tacy.

"Why, she's very nice," said Tib. "Would you be scared, Betsy?"

"Yes, a little," Betsy said.

"I don't see why," said Tib.

"Well," said Betsy. "Let's investigate this lane. And then we can talk some more."

The lane was like a tunnel, green and dim. No clover or butter-and-eggs or daisies grew beneath the beeches. Tacy found some clammy Indian pipes but mostly the grass was empty now. There were traces of a path.

"There's a path here," Betsy said.

"There used to be," said Tib. "But nobody uses it much any more."

"I wonder why not," said Tacy. She said it in a whisper.

"It's leading to something," said Tib excitedly.

"It's so stately," said Betsy looking overhead. "It seems as though it should lead to a Palace."

"It's scary," whispered Tacy. "I'm almost scared to go on."

Betsy was scared too, but she wouldn't admit it. Tib wasn't scared though. Tib was tiny but she was never scared.

"Come on," she said. "There's nothing to be afraid of." And she flew ahead like a little yellow feather. Betsy and Tacy followed, and they came to the end of the lane.

At the end of the lane was the beginning of a house. Just the foundation walls of a house, and it seemed to have been built a long time ago. Tall woolly mullein stalks and blue vervain and sunflowers crowded around the low stone wall which was crumbling and falling away.

"Who do you suppose started that house?" asked Betsy, staring at it.

"And why didn't they finish it?" asked Tacy.

"I'll ask my father," said Tib. "He knows all about houses."

"Oh, no!" cried Betsy. "Let's have this for a secret. We'll call it the Secret Lane."

"We'll say S.L.," said Tacy, "so no one will know what we mean."

"If anyone asks us where we've been today, we'll say we've been to the S.L.," said Tib, dancing about in delight.

"And sometimes we'll say, 'Let's go up to the S.L.,'" said Tacy.

"We'll drive Julia and Katie nearly crazy," Betsy said.

And they all began to laugh, and they scrambled up on the wall. Tib started to walk around it.

"Don't do that, Tib," said Betsy. "These stones are pretty wiggly."

"And this cellar's deep," said Tacy, looking down into the weed-grown soggy place.

But Tib didn't listen to them, and she didn't fall either. She ran on light toes to the back of the cellar wall. When she got there she turned around and came back, so swiftly, so eagerly, that Betsy and Tacy knew she had news.

"Ssh! Ssh!" she said as they drew near.

"What is it?" whispered Betsy and Tacy.

"Just wait 'til you see," Tib replied.

"Do we have to walk on the wall?" asked Betsy.

"No," said Tib. "We can go this way." And she took hold of their hands.

She led them softly around to the back of the house. Reddening sumac bushes crowded close, almost concealing the wall. Tib motioned Betsy and Tacy to pause. They hid themselves in the bushes.

At the back of the house a wing jutted out. A plum tree shaded a little square of ground. And there beneath the plum tree, which was covered with small red balls, sat Julia and Katie.

A fringed blue and white cloth was spread out on the grass. And each girl had a hard-boiled egg in front of her, and a sandwich, and a chunk of cake. Stuck up beside them was a stick and on the stick was a big square card, the same size and shape as that package they always carried to their meetings. It was lettered in large red letters:

BIG HILL MYSTERY CLUB

"Big Hill Mystery! That's B.H.M." Betsy whispered. Tacy and Tib nodded excitedly.

Julia and Katie peeled and salted their eggs. They were having a very serious conversation. They were talking about what they would be when they grew up. Julia thought she would be an opera singer, and Katie thought she would be a nurse.

"Either a nurse or a . . ." began Katie. But just then Betsy moved, and a branch crackled.

"Ssh!" said Julia. "What's that I hear?"

She and Katie looked around.

Behind the sumac bushes Betsy and Tacy and Tib hardly dared to breathe. They scrunched down and waited until Julia and Katie had turned back to their lunch. Then they put their fingers to their lips and pointed to the front of the house. Saying "Ssh! Ssh! Ssh!" and lifting their feet very high, they crept away.

Back in the Secret Lane they hugged one another for joy.

"We know their secret," Betsy said.

"We know where their Club meets," Tacy added.

"We know what B.H.M. means," cried Tib.

They jumped and danced . . . but softly.

"Where shall we eat our lunch?" asked Tacy.

"Right here," said Betsy. "And when they come out from their Club they will see us, and they'll know that we know where their Club meets."

So they sat down and spread out a red and white fringed cloth; and a hard-boiled egg apiece, and a sandwich apiece, and a chunk of cake apiece.

"What's that noise I hear?" asked Tacy as they peeled and salted their eggs.

"Nothing," said Betsy. "They wouldn't be through with their lunch. Let's print the name of our Club on a card and stick it up whenever we meet."

"The Christian Kindness Club! It would look fine," Tacy said.

"I'll print it," said Tib.

While they ate their lunch they had a very serious conversation.

"What shall we do when we grow up?" asked Betsy.

"I'm going to get married and have babies," said Tacy without even thinking.

"I'm going to be a dancer," said Tib, "or else an architect. I haven't made up my mind."

"I'm going to be an author," said Betsy. "And I'm going to look exactly like Aunt Dolly."

"You'll have to get different colored hair," said Tib.

"I know it," said Betsy. "But people do."

"Ssh! Ssh! I hear something," Tacy said.

This time Betsy and Tib heard it too. And they caught the flash of red and blue dresses around the corner of the wall.

"We see you!" they cried, jumping up.

Julia and Katie started to run, and Betsy and Tacy and Tib started to chase them. Tib remembered, though, to pick up the basket and the red and white fringed cloth.

They chased Julia and Katie through the Secret Lane and past Mrs. Ekstrom's house and down the Big Hill. Nobody caught anybody but it was very exciting. Shouting, feet pounding, skirts flying, they ran into Betsy's yard.

Betsy's mother was sitting there with Margaret playing beside her.

"Mercy! What's the matter?" she asked, as they dropped in a heap of waving arms and legs.

"We know where your B.H.M. Club meets!" shouted Betsy, Tacy and Tib.

"We know where your T.C.K.C. meets," Julia and Katie shouted back.

"Big Hill Mystery!" yelled Betsy, Tacy and Tib.

"The Christian Kindness Club!" yelled Julia and Katie.

"You see," said Tacy to Betsy and Tib, "I *told* you someone was there."

Betsy's mother took Margaret on her lap to be out of the way of the waving arms and legs.

"I have a suggestion to make," she said, smiling.

"Since you know all about one another's clubs, and since they both meet up on the Big Hill, why don't you have your meetings together?"

"Together!" cried Julia and Katie and Betsy and Tacy and Tib.

"Go up on the Big Hill together and eat your picnics together. I think it would be fun," Betsy's mother said.

Julia and Katie looked at each other in horror, and Betsy and Tacy and Tib exchanged horrified glances too.

Wasn't that just like a grown-up, thought Betsy, to think that that would be fun?

"You think it over," said Betsy's mother, smiling.

"Yes ma'am," said Julia and Katie and Betsy and Tacy and Tib.

And they thought it over. But the B.H.M. and the T.C.K.C. never met together. Not once.

10

Aunt Dolly

AUNT DOLLY'S train was to reach Deep
Valley at night. Betsy and Tacy would
be in bed and asleep when she arrived.
They wanted to be at Tib's house early the next
morning. So they worked out a plan.

That night when Tacy went to bed, she was to tie
a string to her big toe. She was to let the string hang

out the window. In the morning Betsy would come over and pull the string to wake her up.

"But maybe you won't wake up first, Betsy," Tacy said as she and Betsy climbed the stairs to the little room Tacy shared with Katie.

"That's right," said Betsy. "Maybe I won't. Maybe we'd better tie a string to my toe too."

So after they had poked a string . . . with a stone on one end to make it fall to the ground . . . through a hole in the screen, and tied the other end of the string to the bedpost, awaiting night and Tacy's toe, they crossed the street to Betsy's house. They climbed the stairs to the little room Betsy shared with Julia and poked a string through a hole in *that* screen and tied the other end to a post of *that* bed, awaiting night and *Betsy's* toe. And that night Julia and Katie helped them tie the strings to their big toes. (Julia and Katie were nice sometimes.)

But, as it happened, neither string got pulled.

Tacy had bad dreams and twisted and turned in the night so that the string was wound around her leg and Betsy would have had to stand on stilts to reach it. And Betsy's string came off her toe in the night. But both of them woke up early just the same. They met in the middle of the road.

It was very early; the sky was the color of Betsy's mother's opal ring. The air was cold, and up on the

Hill Street Hill where Betsy and Tacy went to pick flowers for Aunt Dolly, the grass was wet with dew. When their arms were full of goldenrod and bright purple asters, they went down to Hill Street and sat on Tacy's hitching block. It was too early yet to go to Tib's.

"I imagine she'll be beautiful," said Tacy.

"Of course she will," said Betsy. "Remember how her picture looked?"

"It looked like a grown-up doll," said Tacy.

The sun came up higher and higher, and the sky turned a bright gay blue. Smoke began to pour from chimneys, and Grandpa Williams came out to mow his lawn.

"I think we could go to Tib's now," said Betsy.

"We'd better," said Tacy, "or we'll be called to breakfast."

So they skipped down Hill Street and through the vacant lot and rapped at Tib's back door.

Matilda came to the door. She had on an apron and she held a long fork in her hand. She looked busy.

"Tib can't come out yet. She's eating breakfast. There's company," Matilda said.

Betsy and Tacy looked at each other. There was company! Then there hadn't been any mistake.

"It's the company we've come to see," said Betsy.

"We've brought her these flowers," said Tacy.

"We've wiped our feet," said Betsy, and she wiped them again, hard, and so did Tacy.

"Well, wait a minute," Matilda said.

She went through the swinging door into the dining room. Betsy and Tacy waited.

"You can come in," Matilda said when she returned.

They followed her into the dining room. The family was at breakfast there. Tib's father sat at the head of the table with Hobbie in a high chair beside him. Tib's mother sat at the foot. Tib and Freddie sat on one side of the table; and on the other side, facing them, sat Aunt Dolly.

She was more beautiful than her picture. She was more beautiful even than they had imagined her to be. She had blue eyes like Tib's and a pink and white face like a doll's. Her blonde hair was piled in curls on the top of her head.

When Betsy and Tacy entered the room, Tib's face turned red.

"Come in," said Tib's mother in her brisk kind voice. "Matilda says you came to see Aunt Dolly."

"Yes, ma'am," said Betsy. Her face was shining with excitement.

Tacy didn't say a word. She was bashful. Tacy wasn't bashful with Mr. and Mrs. Muller any more, but she was very bashful with Aunt Dolly.

Betsy wasn't bashful exactly, but she felt queer inside.

"We brought her some flowers," she said, nodding toward Aunt Dolly.

Aunt Dolly threw back her head and laughed. She had a little tinkling laugh; it sounded like those bells made of glass and painted with strange flowers which hung on the porch at Betsy's house and chimed when the wind blew.

"Why do you bring flowers to me?" she asked in a tone which showed that she knew the reason perfectly well.

"Because you're so pretty," said Betsy, and everyone laughed.

"That's because I had a grandmother who came from Vienna," Aunt Dolly said, pushing her soft light curls into place.

"Frederick," said Mr. Muller. "Where are your manners? Won't you draw up some chairs for these ladies?"

"Oh," said Betsy. "We didn't come to breakfast."

"Have some coffee cake at least," said Mrs. Muller. "Matilda will put the flowers in a vase."

So Matilda put the flowers in a vase, and Freddie brought chairs, and Betsy and Tacy ate coffee cake and looked at Aunt Dolly. Tib and Freddie looked at Betsy and Tacy. The grown-ups talked about Aunt Dolly's visit, and presently they all finished breakfast and Aunt Dolly stood up.

Betsy and Tacy could see her better then. She was wearing a teagown of pleated white silk, and beneath her small bosom pale blue ribbons were tied.

"I must go to unpack," she said, patting back a yawn with polished fingertips. "Would you children like to come along and see my clothes?"

"Oh, yes," said Betsy and Tacy.

"Freddie can tell your mothers where you are," said Mrs. Muller. "He is going to play with Paul."

So Freddie went off to tell Mrs. Ray and Mrs. Kelly that Betsy and Tacy would be home after a while, and Betsy and Tacy and Tib followed Aunt Dolly to her room.

Her big trunk stood open, and while Betsy and Tacy and Tib watched, entranced, she lifted out her dresses. She certainly had plenty of dresses! There were morning dresses and afternoon dresses; a dress just for horseback riding and a dress just for bicycle riding and lots of ball gowns.

"Dolly!" said Tib's mother, laughing. "Did you forget that you were coming to visit in a small Minnesota town?"

"Oh, I knew you'd like to see them," said Aunt Dolly. "And I like to show them." And she went off to the bureau and moistened her fingers with perfume and touched the lobes of her ears. "Thank you for the flowers, children," she said in a tone which showed that she was ready for them to go.

"You're welcome," said Betsy and Tacy.

"May I go out to play?" asked Tib.

And Betsy and Tacy and Tib went out to the knoll.

"Well," asked Tib when they were seated beneath the oak tree. "What do you think?"

"She's beautiful," said Betsy.

"Do you think she lives in all those crazy places?" asked Tib. "In the Mirror Palace or up in our S.L.?"

"That's what I've been wondering," said Tacy.

Betsy did not answer right away.

"Not any more she doesn't," she said at last.

"What do you mean . . . 'not any more'? I don't understand," said Tib.

Betsy hesitated. It was hard to explain. The truth was that Aunt Dolly was more thrilling being just what she was, than she would be being anything that Betsy could invent. Was that because she was grown-up?

Tacy knew what Betsy was thinking.

"I wonder what it will be like to be grown-up," she said.

"I don't think it will be as nice as being children," said Tib.

"Neither do I," said Tacy. "You don't want to be grown-up, do you, Betsy? At least, not right away."

Betsy sat still for a long moment and thought. She thought about the fun it was being a child. She thought about the Hill Street Hill, and their bench. She thought about the Big Hill and the ravine and the Secret Lane. She looked up into the green shade of the oak tree and thought about the backyard maple.

"No," she answered slowly, "I don't want to be grown-up yet. But I want to be just a little older."

"You're nine already," said Tacy.

"Next year," said Tib, "we'll all be ten."

Betsy jumped up joyfully.

"That's what I'd like to be . . . ten. You have two numbers in your age when you are ten. It's the beginning of growing up, to get two numbers in your age."

Tacy and Tib jumped up too, and they started through the vacant lot.

"But what will we do when we are ten?" asked Tib as they climbed Hill Street Hill.

"I suppose we'll be going to balls," said Betsy. "I'm planning to have a pale pink satin ball gown."

"I'll have a blue one," said Tacy.

"Mine will have a long train," said Betsy.

"I'll carry a big feather fan," said Tacy.

"But we won't be going to balls when we are only ten years old," said Tib.

Tib always said things like that. But Betsy and Tacy liked her just the same.

"We won't be going to balls, maybe," said Betsy. "But we'll have lots of fun, you and me and Tacy."

And so they did.

THE END

Maud Hart Lovelace and Her World

Maud Palmer Hart circa 1906
Collection of Sharla Scannell Whalen

MAUD HART LOVELACE was born on April 25, 1892, in Mankato, Minnesota. Like Betsy, Maud followed her mother around the house at age five asking questions such as "How do you spell 'going down the street'?" for the stories she had already begun to write. Soon she was writing poems and plays. When Maud was ten, a booklet of her poems was printed; and by age eighteen, she had sold her first short story.

The Hart family left Mankato shortly after Maud's high school graduation in 1910 and settled in Minneapolis, where Maud attended the University of Minnesota. In 1917, she married Delos W. Lovelace, a newspaper reporter who later became a popular writer of short stories.

The Lovelaces' daughter, Merian, was born in 1931. Maud would tell her daughter bedtime stories about her childhood, and it was these stories that gave her the idea of writing the Betsy-Tacy books. Maud did not intend to write an entire series when *Betsy-Tacy*, the first book, was published in 1940, but readers asked for more stories. So Maud took Betsy through high school and beyond college to the "great world" and marriage. The final book in the series, *Betsy's Wedding*, was published in 1955.

The Betsy-Tacy books are based very closely on Maud's own life. "I could make it all up, but in these Betsy-Tacy stories, I love to work from real incidents," Maud wrote. "The Ray family is a true portrayal of the Hart family. Mr. Ray is like Tom Hart; Mrs. Ray like Stella Palmer Hart; Julia like Kathleen; Margaret like Helen; and Betsy is like me, except that, of course, I glamorized her to make her a proper heroine." Tacy and Tib are based on Maud's real-life best friends, Frances "Bick" Kenney and Marjorie "Midge" Gerlach, and Deep Valley is based on Mankato.

In fact, so much in the books was taken from real life that it is sometimes difficult to draw the line between fact and fiction. And through the years, Maud received a great deal of fan mail from readers who were fascinated by the question—what is true, and what is made up?

About Betsy-Tacy and Tib

BETSY AND TACY first meet Tib Muller at the end of *Betsy-Tacy*, when the girls are six years old. In real life, however, Maud knew Marjorie Gerlach—or "Midge," as she was called—before then, although they may not really have been friends yet, because they were so young. As Maud remarked: "I have heard from my mother that I had known [Midge] since we were in our baby carriages, for our mothers knew each other." So perhaps it wasn't until the girls were six that they first started to play together. But we do know that by the summer of 1900, when Maud, Bick, and Midge were eight years old, the three girls had become fast friends, just like their fictional counterparts at the beginning of *Betsy-Tacy and Tib*.

Maud and Bick were fascinated by Midge's house, just as Betsy and Tacy are by Tib's. Maud

Collection of Sharla Scannell Whalen

Maud and Bick were fascinated with Midge's house, which stood at 503 Byron Street in Mankato.

once wrote: "Bick and I discovered [Midge's] chocolate-colored house with colored glass over the front door, which to us was a mansion of all glories." Midge's father, who was an architect, like Mr. Muller in the story, apparently designed the Gerlach house. But readers may be surprised to know that although Midge's house *was* brown, and really *did* have a pane of colored glass over the front door, it never had a tower. Instead, it was the house behind Midge's that had a tower, and it is

Although Midge's house didn't really have a tower, Maud may have gotten her inspiration from this house, which stood behind Midge's.

Lois Lenski's drawing of Tib's house

*Henry Gerlach, Midge's father, was
an architect, like Mr. Muller.*

likely this tower that inspired Maud to invent one
for Tib's house.

While Midge's house was a favorite place for in-
door fun, the three girls loved to roam the Big Hill—
which was really Prospect Heights—for outdoor
fun. A Mankato neighbor once described Prospect
Heights in much the same way Maud describes the
Big Hill in the story: "It was a natural playground
for all the children in our neighborhood. On the

other side of the hill was a ravine with a small creek, and on the other side of the creek was Bunker Hill. On the hill and in the ravine, the wildflowers grew in abundance." And there really was a house on the hill, where Anna Asplund lived with her family. Mrs. Asplund was the inspiration for the character Mrs. Ekstrom, who offers sugar cookies to the three hungry beggars at her door.

Many of the episodes in the book, including the

Collection of Bev Schindler

Midge's mother, Minnie Gerlach.

begging episode, were based on real-life incidents. While describing a Thanksgiving dinner reunion with Bick, Maud reminisced: "We talked about old days and laughed very hard about the time we made Everything Pudding and cut off one another's hair." And an old friend of Maud's remembered that "the street carnival was just as it is in the book, flying lady and all." Maud also recalled that Bick played the part of the Flying Lady on the end of a seesaw in the Hart woodshed. Even the mishaps— such as when Bick yelled that she was falling off— are accurately depicted in the book.

Of course, not everything in the book is based on real life. One interesting difference involves Midge's family. Although Midge's brothers, Henry and William, are fictionalized in the books as Freddie and Hobbie, her baby sister, Dorothy, never appears in the books at all. But Dorothy's nickname will be familiar to readers—Maud uses her name for the character Aunt Dolly, who first appears in *Betsy-Tacy and Tib*.

At the end of *Betsy-Tacy and Tib*, the girls wonder what it would be like to be ten. "We won't be going to balls, maybe," Betsy says to Tib. "But we'll have lots of fun, you and me and Tacy." And we can guess that Maud, Bick, and Midge did too.

Maud Hart Lovelace died on March 11, 1980. But her legacy lives on in the beloved series she created and in her legions of fans, many of whom are members of the Betsy-Tacy Society and the Maud Hart Lovelace Society. For more information, write to:

The Betsy-Tacy Society
c/o BECHS
415 Cherry Street
Mankato, MN 56001

The Maud Hart Lovelace Society
Fifty 94th Circle NW, # 201
Minneapolis, MN 55448

Adapted from *The Betsy-Tacy Companion: A Biography of Maud Hart Lovelace* by Sharla Scannell Whalen

THE FINAL SIX BOOKS IN THE BETSY-TACY SERIES

Now Available in Three Volumes, Featuring Original Cover Art by Vera Neville

HEAVEN TO BETSY AND BETSY IN SPITE OF HERSELF
Foreword by Laura Lippman

ISBN 978-0-06-179469-8 (paperback)

Betsy Ray's adventures continue during her freshman and sophomore years at Deep Valley High School, where she discovers a world of new and old friends, Latin and algebra, picnics, parties, and boys! But with her best friends Tacy and Tib, Betsy learns that staying true to herself is the most important lesson of all.

BETSY WAS A JUNIOR AND BETSY AND JOE
Foreword by Meg Cabot

ISBN 978-0-06-179472-8 (paperback)

As Betsy's high school years come to an end, she is positive her junior year will be the best year ever. Things are off to a great start, but soon take a turn for the worse—and Betsy's not sure she can save her perfect year. Then, during her senior year, Betsy must follow her heart and choose between the fascinating, elusive Joe Willard and her longtime friend Tony Markham.

BETSY AND THE GREAT WORLD AND BETSY'S WEDDING
Foreword by Anna Quindlen

ISBN 978-0-06-179513-8 (paperback)

At 21 years old, Betsy sets out on the trip of a lifetime as she begins a solo tour of Europe! Her adventures are endless, and Betsy is determined to make the most of every experience. After her trip is over and she arrives back in New York, Joe Willard is waiting for her—with a marriage proposal Betsy can't refuse.